SYLVIA PLEASE DON'T BE DEAD!

Ann,
I cherish our friendship. Hope this makes you smile!
♡
Stacy

SYLVIA PLEASE DON'T BE DEAD!

STACEY MOLLUS

TATE PUBLISHING
AND ENTERPRISES, LLC

Published by Tate Publishing & Enterprises, LLC
127 E. Trade Center Terrace | Mustang, Oklahoma 73064 USA
1.888.361.9473 | www.tatepublishing.com

Tate Publishing is committed to excellence in the publishing industry. The company reflects the philosophy established by the founders, based on Psalm 68:11,
"The Lord gave the word and great was the company of those who published it."

Cover design by Ivan Charlem Igot
Interior design by Jimmy Sevilleno

Published in the United States of America

ISBN: 978-1-63367-385-4
Fiction / Humorous
15.01.10

ACKNOWLEDGMENTS

I DREAMED OF someday writing an acknowledgments page, but now that I sit down at the computer to compose one, I find it almost impossible because my life has been touched by so many people; my list could easily be longer than this book.

Narrowing it down was tough, but first, I must thank my Lord and Savior, Jesus Christ, who brought me out of a pit and set my feet on a rock. How do I know He lives? Because the moment I gave my life to Him, He changed everything about me, making me a better person than I could have ever have been on my own. To say I am eternally grateful is an understatement.

Second, I want to thank the little red-headed boy that changed my life the second I saw him on the baseball field when we were only fifteen years old—I am so glad you were as adventurous as me and fearlessly asked me to marry you at the ripe old age of seventeen. I love your passion, your protection, and when I am in your arms, everything is perfect. You make my dreams come true.

Next, my three babies who grew into amazing adults—when you were little, I would always tell you to use the gifts God had given you, no matter how many challenges you ran into. I preached to you to "never give up, fight for what you want, and don't let anyone keep you from fulfilling your destiny." Who would have thought as adults, you would give my speech back to me, encouraging me to release this book when I felt much safer just dreaming about it. Like that summer I faced my fears and jumped off the diving board; I needed to do this if I was to "practice what I preached." My love for you has motivated me to face every weakness, only wanting to be the best mom I could be. I can never exhaust the all-consuming love I feel for you.

To those who are my family by law—I want you to know, I could not have handcrafted a family I love more. Marriage may have made us family, but the love we share is supernatural.

Grandma Coy, you were the inspiration for my character, Sylvia. Just like you, she is bigger than life. From dating twins twenty years younger than you, to carrying a gun, to being married so many times, no one in the family knows for sure the real number of spouses you had. You did not allow life to just happen to you; you happened to life. I love the radical faith you received when you made your commitment to God at seventy years old. You took all of that spunky, ornery, hardheadedness and began to use those gifts for good.

Thanks to my momma, who told me from the day I was born, "Be happy, happy, happy"; my dad, who taught me life was a party that I should enjoy; my brothers and sister, who laugh at all the same things I do; my grandkids, who need me to sell this book so I can buy more stickers; my niece, who has lived a lie, forced by me to tell everyone we were sisters so people wouldn't think I was that much older than her; my coworkers, who gave me incredible advice and wisdom, sending me links, e-mails, and words of encouragement; my social media friends, who LOL at my stuff even if it is dorky; my family and friends, who pray for me and speak just the right words at just the right time; Rod McKuen, who showed me when I read his poetry in eighth grade that words can create such incredible feelings, I knew I had to become a writer so I too could motivate people to feel beautiful things; to the driver of the Bookmobile who let me check out a book when I was in the third grade, thus beginning my love of reading; the editors and staff at the St. Joseph News-Press, who gave this unknown, unproven writer her own column in the best women's magazine in the world, *Josephine*; and to all of you who stop me in the grocery store to tell me you enjoy my writing and I really need to write a book, well, this is for every one of you.

I mean this genuinely, I love you all.

CONTENTS

JUST A DAY IN THE LIFE OF MAGGIE

With eyes barely open, Maggie yawned and rolled across her bed to get closer to the window. She snapped back the curtain, hoping the weatherman had been right in his prediction. "Wahoo!" she shouted, seeing the fluffy snowfall which had occurred while she slept. And she loved snow. It made every fiber of her being happy. But then there were not too many things in life that didn't make Maggie, the eternal optimist, happy.

Spring had already sprung in her small hometown, but a strange weather pattern had brought a brief cold snap through the area, leaving a coating of frosty precipitation on the daffodils and tulips, which were already showing their faces for the season.

She laid across her bed, watching the snowflakes swirl and dance in the cold wind. The snow only added to the joy she was feeling on this special day, the eighth anniversary of the day she was hired at The Spot.

The Spot was a little restaurant and grill tucked in the midst of the downtown area. Maggie greatly enjoyed every minute she was there, surrounded by the smell of hamburgers sizzling on the grill and the smiles of the customers she thought of as family. She loved her job and even loved her boss, Mr. Gene, although she may have been the only person in town to admit to a fondness for someone with the personality of a rabid porcupine.

Mr. Gene was rude and gruff and had never married, leading some to believe a lost love may have been the reason for his extreme prickliness, but Maggie saw through all of that. Some days were harder than others to overlook his sour disposition, but during those times, she would just visualize him as a giant toasted marshmallow—crunchy on the outside, a real softy on the inside.

Her admiration for him began long before he became her employer. As a child, Maggie and her parents ate at The Spot every Friday night. While everyone else avoided the grouchy cook, she followed "the man in the white hat and apron" around the restaurant, asking question after question, only to have him grunt his reply. She giggled when he groaned, and she imitated his actions, wiping the counters with napkins and smiling as she watched him cut the crust off of her grilled cheese, just like she liked it.

It may have been her fearlessness or her ability to keep taking his rejection, but something eventually wore him down. He let Maggie into his heart, where no one else had been.

She grew big and so did her fondness for the burly ex-Marine, and that relationship paid its dividend three months after her eleventh birthday when Maggie's mother passed away unexpectedly.

The tragedy had left her and her father financially strapped, a fact Mr. Gene was keenly aware of, so the week after the funeral, he showed up on the doorstep of Maggie's house to speak with her father. Mr. Gene wanted to offer help but also understood a man's pride, so he didn't offer a handout. Instead, he explained to Maggie's father how he was in need of a dishwasher at the restaurant. He explained, "Since Maggie knows the place like the back of her hand, she would require less training than someone off the street."

After negotiations to which Maggie gladly agreed, she started work the next night, standing on a crate so she could reach the faucet. She was thrilled to be working at the "hole in the wall" restaurant she loved, and as she grew, she never had a desire to look for employment anywhere else, believing deeply her purpose for working there was more than just a paycheck. She was Mr. Gene's friend, and to her, that was more important than any big-paying career. She moved up from dishwasher, to fry cook, then to the coveted role she now held, head waitress.

Mr. Gene was not the only reason she loved The Spot. She loved the customers, and they loved her. On more than one occasion, she had been told she was the only reason they still patronized the "greasy spoon ran by such an old coot." Whenever she would hear those things, she would smile and say, "If you only knew him like I do, you wouldn't say such things."

This frost-kissed spring morning, she had extra time to reminisce as her father had left for work long before Maggie had woken up. She ate a bowl full of sugar-and-cocoa-covered cereal puffs and milk, then went back to her room, and grabbed a pair of jeans from the back of the chair and slipped them on. Unsure if the sweatshirt she pulled from the pile of clothes scattered on the floor had made it to the washing machine since her last wearing, she held it up to her nose and gave it a sniff. "Good enough," she said and slipped it over her head. "Now, where are my boots?"

She went to the closet, got down on her knees, and began digging through the years of accumulated items she rotated every time she had to find something that had fallen to the bottom.

After pulling out two boxes of old books, a Little Mermaid sleeping bag she had received as a gift on her tenth birthday, and a ratty purse with a broken zipper, she found the boots underneath the angel costume she had worn in the community Christmas program.

While still on the floor, she crawled around, tossing items that were in her way as she searched for a pair of socks. Under the bed, she found a tall white sock with a blue stripe, and while in search of the mate, she came across a short, yellow sock with lace trim.

Not being one to fret over details and convincing herself, "No one really sees your socks anyway," she slipped on the unmatched combo and proceeded to slide her foot into her boot.

It was met with some opposition about halfway in, so curiously, she pulled the boot back off and bravely stuck her hand into the dark chasm. Her fingers searched around until she felt the offending obstacle, took hold of the mystery object, and pulled out a small gift, wrapped in paper decorated with Christmas trees surrounded by teddy bears in Santa hats. "So, that is where I put that!" she exclaimed.

The sight of the box reminded her of the coin purse inside, which she had bought for her best friend, Sylvia, but was unable to present her with the lovely gift on the appropriate day since she couldn't find it when the time of gift giving approached. In Maggie's mind, it made perfect sense to hide the gift in her boot, just knowing in her heart it would snow on Christmas Eve. That magical snowfall would require her to wear her boots, thus reminding her of her hidden gift. Problem was the dry condition that year did not bring a frosty holiday, and no boots meant hours of searching for the well-hidden gift before giving up and buying a pair of pink, fuzzy house slippers as a last minute replacement. "Gee whiz, I sure hid that good. I guess, a little too good since it was a surprise to even me."

After retrieving the "gift that was yet to be given" from her winter footwear, Maggie placed it on her nightstand, making a mental note to rewrap the gift and give it to Sylvia as a birthday present instead. Without any additional hindrance, she successfully slipped on the boots, grabbed her work uniform and coat, and headed towards the door.

The snow was still falling, and the windshield of her vehicle was covered. She opened the car door, and a glob of snow fell from the top of the vehicle into the truck, leaving a pile of the icy flakes in her seat. "Fiddlesticks," she said.

She slid her hand deep into the sleeve of her puffy, yellow coat and used it as a broom to remove the snow from its unwanted location. Climbing into the car, she reached over and gave her ordinarily stuck glove box a whack, encouraging it to open.

It gave in to her persuasion and laid itself flat. She dug through the crinkled papers and old manuals, looking for an ice scraper but came up empty-handed. "Hmm, wonder where I left that?" she questioned.

Inspecting the seats for the missing scraper, she took her long slender hand and reached it deeply into the crack, pulling out two quarters, a nickel, a mint covered in blue fuzz, and a hard French fry. She put the change in her pocket, tossed the mint and French fry onto the ground, then continued her search.

Maybe, there is something in my purse I could use, she thought, opening her handbag.

"Ah ha!" She reached in and plucked her hairbrush from its location and gave it a new assignment as an ice-removing tool. Using the backside of the hairstyler, she removed the flakes and thin layer of ice from a six-inch circle in the center of the driver's side of the windshield.

"Ready to go." She climbed in and turned the key in the ignition, but the old, beat-up clunker ignored her coaxing and refused to fire up. Maggie pumped the gas pedal and tried again, the car giving a cough from the tailpipe before surrendering to the pressure. Once started, she turned the knob of the defroster to high and pulled away from the curb.

In weather like this, traffic was light, allowing Maggie extra room to maneuver her rusty and dented Oldsmobile through the streets of the city. She was notorious for sideswiping most everything on her block so with the roads a little slick, she appreciated the extra space.

Slipping and sliding down the road, she noticed against the snowy backdrop, a shadowy figure walking along the side of the road. As she got closer, she tapped on the brake to slow down and get a better look. It was Homeless George, the only homeless man in town, therefore easily recognizable.

She saw his gloveless, weathered hands pulling the collar of his tattered coat tightly closed around his neck. She always felt sympathy for him, but seeing him struggling so much against the wind plucked her heartstrings exceptionally hard on this day.

"No gloves? I can change that." Her overactive thoughts of George getting frostbite motivated her to change her plans. She drove up close to the man and yelled out the window, "Morning, George. You stay put! I am going to go and buy you some gloves. I will be right back."

Used to being cursed at by the traveling public, George ignored her directions completely. Maggie never noticed his disobedience as the impulsive U-turn she completed caused the rear end of her vehicle to fishtail. A sudden yank on the steering wheel quickly straightened it out before she traveled the five blocks to Kmart a bit faster than the elements suggested.

Arriving safely, she found a parking spot and sprinted into the store, pulling her own coat closed to be protected from the chill. She stepped inside the building and was just shaking the wet precipitation from her hair when she looked up and noticed a sweet-looking old woman standing in front of her.

Why in the world is this tiny, thin-skinned lady out on a day like today? she thought. Her question was soon answered as she watched the geriatric female heading towards the pharmacy.

"Oh, the poor thing probably had to get out in this weather to buy her life-giving medication."

Taking a few seconds from her homeless-man rescue to help the little angel get her pills seemed like the right thing to do, so Maggie detoured from one mission to assist in another.

Piously, she smiled as she thought, *God must be very proud of me, I know He is watching today as I unselfishly help these people in need.*

She walked up beside the elderly lady, her close proximity causing the woman to stop and look up at her. The wrinkly female smiled a toothless smile, her acknowledgment convincing Maggie that the lady was also feeling that this was a God-ordained moment.

Demurely, Maggie batted her eyes and spoke softly to "Miss Wrinkly," "Bless you, dear." She humbly lowered her head and reached out her arm to take hold of the elderly female, hoping to escort her into the presence of the pharmacist. As she slipped her hand through the crook of the lady's arm, she was unaware her hand had also accidently ran through the strap of the woman's purse.

Having seen one to many reports of crime rings on *Dateline*, a growl began to grow in the old woman's wrinkly little soul and work its way up and out of her mouth. She planted her tiny feet and curled her bony, arthritic fingers into a fist and began to quiver.

Maggie looked at her and asked, "Are you having a seizure? It is your lucky day because I happen to know CPR."

The wrinkly one snarled then began struggling to pull away. Maggie abruptly released her grip of the older woman, but as she stepped away, the purse caught on the button of her coat sleeve. With the separation complete, Maggie slowly lifted her arm, and there hung the old lady's property.

The ladies looked at each other, then at the purse, then again at each other. Miss Wrinkly took a karate stance and let out a guttural sound. Maggie panicked and, out of fear for her life, turned to run.

The old woman was not about to let her purse go without a fight, so just like a flying monkey, she leapt onto Maggie's back and held on for dear life.

Maggie began spinning in circles as she tried to break the grip of the freakishly strong geriatric. "Why are you doing this to me?" she questioned. "I am here on a mission, and you are squeezing my carotid artery! Please stop doing that, or I am going to have to stop helping you."

The centrifugal force of their circular motion shook the purse loose, and it fell to the floor. Miss Wrinkly slid off of Maggie's back and began screaming, "Purse thief! Helllp!"

People turned and looked towards the scene that the loud woman was making. Maggie bent down, picked up the purse, and shoved it into the lady's hand, saying loud enough for the spectators to hear, "It's all right, honey. You just dropped your purse, but I have gotten it for you now. You poor little thing."

Going one step further to convince the crowd she wasn't a purse snatcher, she threw her arms around Miss Wrinkly and began to hug her like she was a long-lost aunt. She could feel the tiny body squirming in her bear hug, but she did not let go, mainly because the woman's face shoved into Maggie's chest muffled the cursing coming from the deceptively sweet little lady. As the crowd dispersed, Maggie loosened her grip, and Miss Wrinkly stepped back.

Assuming an apology would be forthcoming, Maggie stood and waited, but instead a sinister grin began to creep across the age-worn face of the old lady as she took hold of a stray shopping cart. She curled her fingers tightly around the handle, turned towards Maggie, and began scraping her feet on the floor like a bull that had spotted a bright red cape in the hand of the matador.

Maggie realized she was about to become the target of a shopping cart torpedo. She turned to walk away, the elderly assassin following close behind. Maggie picked up her pace from a brisk walk, to trotting, to running for her life.

She turned down the toy aisle and dove behind a Tickle Me Elmo display to hide. She took a deep breath and held it until the squeaky cart driven by the demented grandmother went flying past her.

Good thing her eyesight is not as good as it was forty years earlier, or I could have become a speed bump! Maggie thought.

The sound of tiny shuffling feet got softer as they moved off into the distance. Maggie slowly peeked around the rack of stuffed animals and saw Wrinkly heading down the aisle.

Once the coast was clear, she made her break. She ran towards the accessory department, weaving in and out of the aisles in case Miss Wrinkly came back for her prey. Grabbing the first pair of gloves she saw, she made it safely to the cashier. Her foot began tapping nervously once she saw the security camera in the corner of the retail store. *What if they really think I am a mugger? What if they take me in for a police lineup and that old lady IDs me as a purse snatcher?* Her panic was interrupted by the cashier asking for the cash to complete the purchase. Maggie fumbled her debit card as she quickly swiped it thru the reader. She snatched her receipt from the worker, grabbed the gloves, and headed out the door.

Stepping off the curb, she noticed movement in her peripheral vision. She spun her head around, and there was her archnemesis Miss Wrinkly. Braving the cold, the aged woman had hidden behind the soda machine until Maggie came out of the store.

Her cheeks were red from the cold, her aged nostrils flared, and she had rolled up her sleeves, ready to rumble. Maggie took a long look at the woman and thought, *How in the world can this little birdlike human with scrawny little arms look so intimidating?*

Realizing she was under attack, she had no choice but to take off running again. The only sounds she could hear were the lady's cart rolling behind her and her maniacal laugh getting louder as she got closer. Maggie was running out of steam, her breath short and strained. She looked over her shoulder at the face of her adversary, suddenly closing in on her.

She devised a quick plan, which involved the risky move of slowing down to entice her attacker into the trap. This was a risky move due to the super-human agility of the senior citizen, but she had no choice. This would either save her or be her demise.

Just as the dusty diva was about to catch her prey, Maggie leapt into action. A quick swerve to the left and a slight turn sideways, Maggie slid between the building and the electronic merry-go-round, and kept moving. She ran about six more steps and heard the crash she had hoped for.

The shopping cart, being too wide to fit through the narrow passageway, wedged between the spinning pink unicorn and the cement wall of the building.

The puny perpetrator raised her fist and began yelling curses towards Maggie, who never looked back. She just kept running until she reached her vehicle. She yanked on the handle, jumped inside, and locked the door behind her, just in case.

Pulling from the parking lot, Maggie was still winded from the chase. She watched in the rearview mirror as the elderly stalker ran behind the truck for a full block before giving up. "Boy, that woman is in good shape!" Maggie said aloud as she finally gained enough distance to feel safe. Back to her original mission, she slowly drove down the street where she had previously seen George, looking around and between the buildings. About to give up, she rounded the curve on the boulevard, and there was the man in need.

She turned on her blinker and gave her steering wheel a sharp tug, cutting across three lanes of traffic. The vehicle weaved out of control. She slammed on the brakes, hit the curb, and did a donut before coming to rest directly in front of the startled homeless man. He jumped back in fright.

She threw open her car door and jumped out.

He screamed, "Please don't hurt me!"

Maggie did not hear his pleas as she was thinking, *This must be what Mother Teresa felt like when she did all of her good deeds.* She spoke to George, "I am not here to harm you. I am here to help you. I noticed you had no gloves, so I sacrificed and went out of my way to get you a pair. You should know, I was almost killed by an elderly woman while trying to buy these, but there is no need to thank me."

She held out the gloves with both hands and bowed, looking as if she was presenting a gift to a king.

"Get away from me, you crazy woman!" he shouted, then took off running.

Maggie took off right behind him. Her energy had been previously spent trying to save her own life, and she was still a bit worn out, so he got away pretty quickly. It did not take long for her to realize she was not going to catch him.

With the little air she had left in her lungs, she yelled, "Come back here and take these stinking gloves I bought for you! I love you with the love of God, doggone it!"

He never even looked back.

As he faded into the daytime, she turned and headed back to her car as a police cruiser whipped in beside Maggie's vehicle.

"*Freeze!* Step away from the vehicle!" The officer pulled his gun from its holster as he stepped from his vehicle. "Maggie? Is that you?"

"Good morning, Officer Larry. What are you doing here?" She was oblivious to the weapon pointing in her direction. She continued speaking, "I have been kind of busy this morning. I went out and bought homeless George a pair of gloves, but I guess he had somewhere he had to get to fast because he sure took off like a rocket."

The officer shook his head and put away his gun. This was not the first time he had been called to the scene and found Maggie involved in a false alarm. Knowing he already had his answers, he still had to ask, "We just had a call come into the station. Someone reported an 'attempted assault with a vehicle.' Can you tell me anything about that?"

"Well, that is weird because I have been out here for a bit, and I didn't see anyone trying to run over some innocent soul. People these days are crazy," Maggie replied.

Officer Larry shook his head in disbelief then said, "How about you take it a little easy today, with the slick roads and all."

"You betcha!" Maggie said, climbing into her car. She started to pull away, giving a big wave to the policeman. She smiled as she passed by, drove up over the curb, almost hit the patrol car, but, after straightening it out, headed in the direction of the diner.

WAKING UP IN THE MORNING… ALWAYS A GOOD THING

Across town, Sylvia picked up her glasses from the nightstand and maneuvered them around the curlers she had placed in her short gray hair the night before. She spun her legs around and dangled them off the side of the bed before making the same declaration she made every morning before her feet hit the floor, "Good morning, world. It's gonna be a good day today because I have a pulse!" She felt the need to reiterate that each day, because at seventy years old, waking up was not something she took lightly.

She slipped her brightly painted red toenails into her slippers and headed to the kitchen. Turning the burner on, the stove allowed the gas to escape with a hiss as she reached into the cabinet, took a wooden match, and struck it firmly. Nearing the burner with the fire, it met with the gas and flames shot up. She placed her rooster-shaped teapot on top of the burner, and in a very short time, the liquid in the porcelain poultry came to a boil. Two scoops of instant coffee were dumped into a mug decorated with big letters that read "One Hot Mama" before she poured the boiling water over the crystals. She gave it a good, long stir, the spoon clanging against the side of the mug with each rotation. Sitting the cup on the table to brew, she headed to the front porch to get the newspaper.

"Good morning, Mr. Newsome," she said as she spotted the elderly bachelor who lived next door. She stood a little taller and sucked in her protruding tummy then took her hands and ran them over her rollers, tucking in the stray hairs.

"Well, good morning to you, Miss Sylvia," he said, tipping the bill of his hat in her direction. "Got your rollers in? Must mean you're goin' to town today."

"Yes, sir, I am. Got me a list as long as my arm of things I need to do today," she replied.

He took his pruning shears and snipped off one of his prized hybrid T-roses he had growing in front of his house and walked over to her porch. "For you, madam," he said, handing her the beautiful blossom.

She took the flower and held it up to her nose and sniffed it. "You, sweet talker, you. Keep that up and I am going to have to bake you another one of my lip-smacking raisin pies."

"I would surely love one, but you can save yourself all of that work by just givin' me a little smooch right here," he said, pointing to his smoothly shaved cheek.

"Mr. Newsome! What kind of lady do you think I am? You have to get this nonsense out of your head. I told you,

I am not looking for husband number eight right now. You better behave yourself." She picked up her newspaper, gave him a flirty wink, then turned and went back into the house.

Leaning as far as his old bones would let him, just to catch one last glimpse of Sylvia as she walked into her house, a huge grin crossed his face as he went back to pruning his roses.

Sylvia sat down at the kitchen table, put the coffee cup to her lips, and blew before taking a big swig. "Well, will you look at that?" she said to Jake, her lazy mixed-breed terrier who was her constant companion.

Reading from the newspaper's headlines, she elaborated, "Old man Simpson's kid is running for sheriff. I tell you right now, that family is as honest as the day is long. I knew this boy's great-grandma. She had a stand on the corner of Ashland and Noyes where she sold tomatoes every summer. Best I ever did eat. And you know what? She always set her scale a hair below zero, so you always knew you were getting more than what you paid for. Yep, honest folks they are. I am going to have to call the girls in my water aerobics class and tell them they need to vote for this boy. Gotta get some truth back in that office. He is the complete opposite of that devil they got in there now. I know for a fact that punk's great-uncle, Bud, was a moonshiner. And not even a good one! His hooch tasted like turpentine, and you know, the nut don't fall far from the tree. If his great-uncle was a shyster, so is that boy."

Jake looked up from his bowl of table scraps she had served him and tilted his head to the right as if he was contemplating her ravings.

She closed the paper and returned to the stove to cook her breakfast. Taking the old coffee can from the counter containing the bacon drippings she always saved, she poured some into a skillet and cracked an egg on the side of the pan, dropping it into the hot oil. The egg immediately began to sizzle.

As Sylvia took the spatula and splashed the grease upon the egg, it quickly turned white. Not allowing them to sit in the oil for long so the yolks remained runny, she tilted the pan over her plate, and the slimy masterpiece easily slid onto it.

She put the skillet in the sink, turned off the fire, then sat back down at the table. She sliced off a piece of her homemade bread and dipped it into her coffee, pausing long enough for it to soak up the now lukewarm liquid. She popped the sloppy concoction into her mouth, using her fork to chop her eggs into little bitty pieces before consuming them. After her stomach was full and the dishes washed up, she looked at Jake and said, "Let's go get dolled up!"

It was the first of the month, and her pension check had arrived. On payday, she dressed up and took the bus into town to do some shopping and catch up on the latest gossip at The Spot. Occasionally she would meet up with friends and have lunch, but mainly she enjoyed the company of Maggie who she considered her best friend.

Sylvia went into the bedroom and pulled one of her nicest dresses from the closet, laying it on the bed. She reached into the back of her underwear drawer and pulled out her lone brassiere, the one that only came out on special occasions and paydays.

Time and gravity had taken its toll on the very busty woman who never wore a bra, but a couple of misplaced body parts did not affect Sylvia's ultra-high self-esteem. Even after being questioned naively by her great-grandson as he sat on her lap, "Great-grandma, where are your breasts?" She calmly answered, "They are in my lap, young man." Nothing more was ever uttered.

She pulled the bra around her, snapped it in the front, then began the exhausting feat of turning it around so the snaps would finish in the back. "I swear, Jake, you are so lucky you don't have to wear one of these things. I tell you, bras are the reason so many women have digestive problems. You cannot cut off the blood flow to the stomach with these contraptions and not have problems."

She grabbed the bra with both hands and pulled it one direction as she twisted her body the opposite way, looking as if she was trying desperately to free herself from the grasp of a python. Once her mammaries were hoisted into place, she sat down on the edge of the bed to catch her breath. Taking the back of her hand, she wiped the sweat that had formed on her brow, then stood up and slipped her dress over her head, buttoning the three buttons that held it closed.

Standing before the mirror on her dresser, she removed the rollers from her hair, took a wide-toothed comb, and ran it through the little white ringlets, smoothing them into a style. She finished off her look by patting her face gently with a powder puff and adding a coat of ruby red lipstick to finish her makeover. Coincidently, the lipstick came out on the same occasions as the brassiere.

There was one last accessory Sylvia was never without—her .38-caliber Colt revolver. She had won the gun in a poker game one hot summer night, twenty-five years before, and from that day on, she was never unarmed. She carried it in her purse during the day and slept with it under her pillow at night.

Whenever questioned about it, her disappointment was apparent when she spoke about only being able to pull it on two men since she became a "gun-toting" woman. Her second husband was the first she took aim at when she found him with another woman; the second was an inebriated young man who she caught leaning against her house, throwing up in the wee hours of the morning. All it took was the site of her gun, pointed at his head through her window screen, to help him suddenly feel well enough to move on down the road.

Tucking her gun safely in her purse, she took one last look in the mirror and informed Jake, "You are in charge of the house while I am gone." He never even lifted his head to acknowledge her exit. She pulled the door shut and double-checked the lock before walking to the bus stop.

HUBBA, HUBBA, THERE'S A NEW GUY IN TOWN

THE BUS CAME to a halt in front of the restaurant, and Sylvia stepped off. Opening the door of the eating establishment, the familiar smell of grease hit her in the face. After a stroll across the red-and-white tiled flooring of the dining area, she took a seat on the barstool at the counter.

Maggie had also just arrived and was tying her starched-white apron around her skinny waist. She grabbed a pencil and stuck it behind her ear before picking up a menu and filling a big glass with Dr. Pepper in anticipation of Sylvia's request.

"Don't you just love this weather?" Maggie squealed as she sat the cold drink in front of her friend.

"Not just no, but *heck* no!" Sylvia replied. "I would much rather be baking in the summer sun wearing my polka-dot bikini. I mean, seriously, wearing all of these bulky layers? How am I supposed to show off my assets to the menfolk if they are buried underneath a pile of clothing?" She gently cupped her breasts and bounced them up and down a couple times to emphasize her point. She grabbed the menu and looked it over, quickly making her decision, "I will have the chicken fried steak, fried potatoes, and wilted greens with bacon fat dressing."

Concerned for Sylvia's health, Maggie made a suggestion, "Maybe you could consider a grilled chicken breast with a salad instead."

"You can keep your rabbit food." Sylvia replied. "My doctor barks at me all the time, saying I shouldn't eat like this, but I tell you, my granny ate like this her whole life, and she lived to be 101 years old. All that grease in her diet kept her joints lubed up, and she got around better than you."

She took a sip of her soda before continuing, "Shoot, when she was the ripe old age of seventy-two, she caught granddaddy talking with the widow women that lived next door. Granny was up and over that fence faster than a squirrel up a tree! She grabbed that hussy by her dyed-red hair and took her to the ground. Granny made her point then climbed back over the fence. She brushed the wrinkles from her skirt, grabbed granddaddy by the suspenders, and led him back up to the house. The old widow woman moved out of that house within the month. I'm telling you, grease is good. It saved Granny's marriage."

As Sylvia continued explaining to Maggie the benefits of lard, two nicely-dressed men came into the diner. They looked around the place and then took a seat in the open booth by the window. Maggie excused herself from Sylvia's conversation to present the strangers with glasses of water and menus.

"Good morning, fellas. Welcome to The Spot. Can I get you something to drink?" Maggie asked, as she pulled her order pad from her pocket.

The men looked focused on their conversation, and her presence seemed to be a distraction, but the younger of the two turned his head and looked up at Maggie. When his chocolate-brown eyes met hers, she instantly went weak in the knees.

"I think we both want iced tea," he said, but she didn't really hear a word he'd spoken. She blinked several times, trying to focus on the beautiful man sitting in front of her, but no matter how many times her eyelids opened and closed, the room still looked fuzzy to her.

Leaving them with their menus, she slowly made her way back to the counter where Sylvia was seated. She stood frozen in place like a wooden soldier.

Sylvia asked, "Are you okay? You look like you are going to throw up! If you are, let me know right now because I am a sympathetic puker. If I see you blow chunks, I am going to spew right beside you."

Sylvia began gagging. "See? Now I'm going to throw up." She grabbed a menu and started fanning herself.

The air flow she stirred up brought Maggie back to reality while also calming Sylvia's gag reflex.

Maggie explained, "I don't think I am going to throw up, but I am feeling a bit strange. My legs are all wobbly, and I feel clammy. I think that man over there gave me some instant rare disease." She took a napkin from the dispenser and blotted her forehead before continuing, "It was so odd. I just looked into his beautiful, dreamy eyes and…see, there it is again! It feels like the earth's rotation has slowed down, and it makes me dizzy." She sprawled her upper torso across the counter and laid her face flat against the cool surface.

Her hypochondria kicked in, and she sat straight up. "Oh no! Maybe I'm coming down with something life threatening." She leaned forward, took Sylvia's hand, and slapped it against her own forehead. "Do I feel like I have a fever to you? I heard the swine flu is going around, and I bet you a dollar, I caught it!"

She dropped Sylvia's hand and felt her forehead, trying to determine her body temperature. "I better call Daddy and have him meet me at the hospital."

Sylvia spun her stool around and gazed at the very handsome man Maggie had pointed out. One look and she figured out Maggie's disease. "Girl, you don't have the pig flu, but I do think you got bit by a bug, the love bug!" She giggled at her friend's innocence.

"Love bug? Is there a shot for that because I really hate shots." She leaned against the counter as the color left her face. "I think I am going to pass out! I'm starting to see sparkles."

"You're not getting a shot," Sylvia firmly stated.

"No shot?"

"No."

"Thank goodness," she said, the pink slowly returning to her cheeks.

"Now if you will listen, I will tell you about the love bug," Sylvia spoke with authority.

"I am an expert on this subject because I have been bitten at least fourteen times in my life. One would think I would have built up a tolerance to its powers, but I guess you can't become immune to this type of bug."

She took another drink of her soda then continued, "Listen to my words, young one. You got the hots for that boy, and as I check him out"—Sylvia strained to get a better look—"he is not wearing a ring, so I say its game on! A girl has to take what she wants. If I would have been as naive and shy as you are, I would have never gotten married once, let alone seven times. Shoot, husband number five would not have ever noticed me had I not pursued him aggressively. I mean, he was a Pentecostal minister for goodness sake. They are trained to not even look at women!"

As Maggie composed herself, Sylvia stated her example, "I tell you, the night I went into that tent revival and saw that gorgeous man of God on stage, preaching, I knew he would be my next husband." She began fanning herself with the menu again, not to prevent throwing up this time, but because the thought of her ex-husband was giving her a rise in body temperature.

Maggie covered one eye and looked across the room to make sure her vision was clear and her odd feelings were not caused by a stroke while Sylvia continued talking.

"Since it was against his religion to lust, I had to come up with a plan to get him to notice me without appearing to be a harlot. So one not-so-fateful night, I "accidentally" walked out of the choir dressing room and into his office, wearing only a Victoria's Secret bra and panty set. All I can say is, after seeing me in that skimpy outfit, we had a romantic three-week courtship, followed by a beautiful church wedding."

She continued, "Who knows? I might still be organizing ladies events for the congregation if not for that lousy old lady Johnson! She was the dried-up old troll in charge of the sewing circle at the church, and she never did like me because I had all the va-va-voom, and she had the personality of a pit bull with PMS. I knew the first day I met her that she was a snake-in-the grass, so I tried really hard to keep her close, which wasn't easy since she had breath that smelled like butt. I managed to protect myself from her evilness for about two years, then one day, she found one itty-bitty, tiny secret about me and shared it with the world, creating a giant scandal."

Sylvia felt the need to relive the trauma, and since Maggie was still unable to walk, she was a captive audience, so Sylvia continued, "I mean, sneaking out to the bar owned by my fifth husband to do some innocent singing and entertaining was no sin. I tithed on my tips, and I also added 'Amazing Grace' to my song list. Add to that, I was sleeping with the man, so what else did I need to do to receive his blessing? Being a firm believer in 'it's better to ask for forgiveness than permission,' I made up a story about going downtown to feed the homeless to explain why I was gone from home so much. It was a perfect plan, and it had been working for weeks until that mean old noisy woman 'volunteered' to help me. I told her this was my 'personal' calling, and she needed to go find her own mission, one that her face was more suited for, like scaring away rats in the alley. But she refused to go away. Then one night, she and three of her vulture friends trailed me and found out I was not feeding anyone. They saw just enough of my second act to declare me a harlot, and the old bats flew back to their cave and wasted no time reporting my secret activities to the Right Reverend. I don't know who was more shocked that night, me or my naive husband, when he threw open the door of the bar and found me, his adoring wife, lying across the bar, wearing a corset and feather boa and singing my heart out."

She got a faraway look in her eyes as she remembered that moment, then shook it off, and continued, "None of that should matter to you, Maggie. The point is, you have to go after what you want, and I am just the lady to help you do just that. Here is what we are going to do. I will eat my lunch in the booth behind those nice gentlemen. You will come over and be a 'charming waitress,' and when you are taking their orders, you and I will begin a conversation, full of brilliant banter. The young man you are all worked up about will hear how interesting you are, and he will have no choice but to invite you on a date to get to know you better. And who knows"—she pointed to herself as she finished—"maybe the older gentleman with him might like to take this eligible bachelorette out for a spin."

There was no room for debate, as Sylvia had already scooped up her Dr. Pepper, purse, and silverware, and headed over to her new lunch location.

Maggie needed a moment to collect her thoughts, so she headed to the back of the restaurant to compose herself. *What in the world am I allowing Sylvia to get me into this time?* she questioned. *I am not about to go out there and embarrass myself in front of that adorable specimen of manliness. I mean, I bet he already has a girlfriend, and they are going to run off to Vegas and get married by an Elvis impersonator or something. I'm sure he is so in love, he won't even notice I have a face when I go back to his table. Yep, I will be the faceless waitress.* She made herself giggle at her own wittiness.

She peaked out into the dining area and saw Sylvia sitting directly behind the handsome stranger. Her eyes passed quickly over Sylvia and locked on to who she really wanted to see.

His hair looks as soft as a new kitten, she thought, swallowing hard as she tried to gain the courage to proceed.

She looked in the mirror and felt terribly inadequate; her hair in complete disarray. *My goodness, I look like a hay bale shot out of a cannon!*

She turned on the faucet and ran her fingers under the water, using the moisture to stroke her hairline in an attempt to plaster down the strays that always worked their way out of her ponytail holder. She pinched her cheeks to give them color, which was really unnecessary as they were already glowing from the thought of actually conversing with this man. She leaned closer to the mirror and smiled, checking her teeth for any leftover remnants of the bagel she had eaten earlier. Lastly, she pulled the straps on her bra a little tighter, hoping to give the appearance of cleavage but to no avail. Deciding that was as good as it was going to get, she gave herself a little pep talk.

Okay, girl, you can do this. You are hot and sexy. Men everywhere desire you…oh, who am I kidding! She took a deep breath and headed back out to the dining area.

YOU WOULD THINK BAD GUYS WOULD BE MORE DISCREET

Sylvia, knowing her hearing was not what it used to be, positioned herself in the booth to get a better angle on the conversation. She turned her body slightly sideways but did not stay there for long as her ample body was wider than the space between the table and the back of the booth. She wiggled and squirmed, trying to get turned back around, desperate to hear the conversation that was beginning to get juicy.

"You mean, she is that old and still lives alone?" the more aged man asked with excitement. "This is going to be a breeze. We can sneak up on her, and she'll never even know what hit her. It'll be like shooting fish in a barrel."

The younger man replied, "Exactly! You know as well as I do, the family will be so glad we did this. They will be shouting with joy. Each and every one of them has thought about doing it themselves, but they never had the nerve."

Continuing with the details, the young man added, "She is very hard of hearing, so we should have no problem sneaking in, but I will have to come up with a good story to tell the neighbors so they don't get nosey and start snooping round and blow our cover. Plus I don't want them to freak out when they hear the explosions. We sure don't want them calling the police."

Startled by what she had just heard, Sylvia flinched and shook the table, causing her drink to tip over. The sticky carbonated liquid poured onto the Formica surface then onto the floor.

She gave a halfhearted attempt to clean it up by laying a couple tiny paper napkins on top of the spill, her focus more on the men and their plan than good housekeeping.

The older man spoke, "So where exactly does your grandma live?"

"She lives on the corner of third and Locust in a big two-story Victorian house."

Sylvia's eyes widened. She knew immediately who he was talking about. Their target was widow woman Jensen.

He continued, "She has lived in that big old house since she was a child. Her parents left her the property when they died. She went on to marry my grandfather, and they had only the one child, my father, whom you know. My grandfather died several years ago, and he left her very well off. She could live another one hundred years and still not out run out of money!"

Sylvia was taking mental notes. She had a feeling the moment she laid eyes on the two men they were no good, but she had no idea she would be overhearing them plotting a crime. *He must be the ultimate scum to try and knock off his own grandmother for her money,* she thought.

While Sylvia continued eavesdropping, Maggie had gotten up the nerve to come out from the back. She balanced the drinks the men had ordered on her serving tray and headed to their table. Desperately trying to appear confident, her thoughts and emotions were going in opposite directions.

Don't trip, her thoughts reminded her, *don't say anything stupid, and try to look sophisticated.*

She held her head high and began walking toward the table where the men were sitting. The younger man looked up from his conversation and smiled as she got closer. She felt like she was floating, but the truth was she had just put her foot down in the puddle of brown liquid that had originated from Sylvia's table.

She tried to catch herself, but the violent shift forward and then backward took her off her feet. She came down with a thud; the drinks she was carrying shattering on the floor beside her. The diner became silent except for the sound of the drink tray which was wobbling in circles on the floor.

The young man jumped from his seat and helped Maggie sit up. "Are you okay?" he asked. She took a moment to reply, her thoughts scrambled from the impact of her head hitting the floor. Dizzy, she took her hand and gently touched the back of her head, feeling the knot that had already began forming.

"Do you need a doctor?" the young man asked.

She slowly turned her head to look into his face, and as her eyes focused, she smiled adoringly.

He bent down in front of her, put his hands under her arms, then began lifting her to her feet. She wanted to stand, but her legs felt like wet noodles, not from the fall, but because she'd never had a boy this close to her before, let alone had one put their arms around her. She hung in his grasp like a rag doll.

Mr. Gene, having heard the commotion, appeared on the scene. Determining from a quick visual inspection that her injuries were not life-threatening, he said in his gruff voice, "I am going to have to dock your pay for laying down on the job unless you get up right now. People do not want to come into a fancy establishment like this one and see their server squirming around on the floor. Clean up this mess before someone gets hurt." He turned and headed back to the kitchen.

She looked up at the handsome, dark-haired stranger, her ponytail and apron both slightly askew, and stammered, "I'm s-s-so, s-s-so sorry. I don't know what just happened."

Sylvia knew exactly what happened and quickly slid out of her booth. She walked behind Maggie and discreetly kicked the napkin she had dropped on the puddle of soda earlier under the table to hide the evidence. She said, "Honey, we all know you are not the most graceful person in the world. Don't blame yourself. You can't help it. You were just born klutzy."

The young man let go of the somewhat unstable Maggie and introduced himself, "My name is Bradley. This is one of my father's business associate, Mike." He pointed at the middle-aged man, who was snacking on his sixth package of saltines from the basket on the table.

She giggled uncomfortably and looked to the floor as she shook Bradley's hand. Sylvia, armed with the newfound revelation of his intentions, interrupted and began nudging Maggie towards the kitchen. "It is very nice to meet you, but if you will excuse us, Maggie here forgot, uh, to get me some, um, sugar substitute. Maggie, could you show me again where that is located? You know, with my eyesight, I get confused between the pink packages and the blue ones." And with that, she gave Maggie a shove towards the back of the restaurant.

"What are you doing?" Maggie asked with a great deal of confusion and frustration after Sylvia had abruptly relocated her to a quiet place. "You always told me you wouldn't be caught dead using a sugar substitute, and why in the world would you start now, just as I was talking to my new friend Bradley."

Sylvia stretched her neck to see around the corner, wanting to keep an eye on the men as she began explaining her behavior, "We are in the presence of criminals, I tell you. Real live hardened criminals. These are some bad men."

The fog had finally left Maggie, and she was in her right mind, but now she was concerned about Sylvia's state. She gently took hold of Sylvia's arm to calm her and asked, "You seem to be a little confused right now. Do you have some kind of pill you need to take that maybe you forgot this morning?"

Sylvia yanked her arm from Maggie's grasp and firmly said, "I don't take any pills! My mind is sharper than anyone in this building. I am telling you, while you were in the back room, I overheard those two men talking about snuffing someone out!"

Maggie needed clarification. "When you say 'snuff out,' what exactly do you mean?"

"What do I mean? Haven't you ever watched *Cops*?" Sylvia said with a huff. "Snuff out. You know, put a hit on, put them on ice, give them a dirt nap. I don't know if I can make it any clearer."

"What in the world would make you think such a thing?"

"I didn't just think such a thing. I heard such a thing!" Sylvia looked around the kitchen to make sure they were alone, then she leaned in to give Maggie the scoop. "The younger male is related to Mrs. Jensen, and I heard him tell the other guy they are going to kill her for her money."

"No!" Maggie gasped.

"Yep, they are going to set off some kind of explosion. And that Bradley character," she said snidely, "told the other man that her whole family disliked her so much, they would be thrilled that they did it! Now in his defense, I used to be a bingo caller at the Legion, and Mrs. Jensen came in every Tuesday night, and she was a pain in the rear. Always whining and complaining about everything from it being too cold to accusing me of cheating because I didn't call the numbers she wanted. She is as irritating as underwear that is too tight, but I would have never guessed all of her kinfolk would want her gone."

Maggie sat down on a big plastic container full of pickle slices. "Boy, I guess you can't tell the good guys from the bad guys anymore."

"Handsome men make the best criminals," Sylvia warned. "They can get by with murder because people get all starry eyed and don't see the evil that's lurking in their soul."

"What should I do? They are sitting in my section, and if I don't get back out there, Mr. Gene is going to be the one to commit a crime. I guess we should call the police right away." Maggie said, before getting up and taking hold of the telephone receiver that hung on the wall.

"No way!" Sylvia said firmly, snatching the phone from Maggie's hand and hanging it up forcefully. "If we go to the police right now, they will think we are just two girls who are freaking out. No one will take us seriously." She stopped for a moment, her mind deep in thought.

"Here is the deal. If we crack this case, they will probably give us some big reward since Mrs. Jensen is rich. I think we should try and get more information before we go to the cops. Those fellas out there don't have a clue I am on to them, so let's go back out there and see what else we can find out. I will go back to my seat, and you need to pump them for information."

"This is freaking me out," Maggie said. "I have never been around a real live criminal before. Well, unless you count my uncle Ernie. He had been arrested so many times for being drunk in public, the police just stopped picking him up. They would just call Aunt Eleanor and make her go get her drunken husband. He was a happy drunk though. A lot of fun."

"Enough about Ernie," Sylvia said. "We need to get back out there before they get suspicious. I'm heading out, and you need to follow me."

"I think that perhaps" Maggie spoke up, hoping to change the plan, but it was too late. Sylvia was already wedged back in the booth, straining to hear every word the men were saying.

Maggie put on a brave face, slowly heading back into the dining area. Doing all she could to stall having conversation with the alleged criminals. She took a mop from the back and cleaned the soda spill, delivered a plate of ham 'n' beans to an over-the-road trucker who was sitting at the counter, gave some extra napkins to a table where a family with a very messy toddler was eating, and refilled the water glasses at another table. Unable to find anything else to keep her from confronting the men, she took a deep breath and walked over to the scary strangers.

"My apologies for the earlier excitement. Nothing like a little entertainment with your lunch, huh?" She chuckled, hoping to appear charming and not freaked out. "So have you decided what you would like to order?" she asked the men.

While Maggie had the attention of the men captured, Sylvia pulled her compact from her purse and held it up a few inches from her face, slowly moving it around until she could easily see the reflection of the men sitting behind her. She made a mental checklist of their characteristics, assuming she would need to identify them in a police lineup later. *Young man, approximately twenty-two years of age, dark hair and eyes, no facial hair or obvious tattoos. Middle-aged man, black wavy hair, no wedding ring, expensive suit with a tie that doesn't quite match his shirt, proving he is single.* While still holding the mirror in place, she took her other hand, removed her pistol from her purse, and softly laid it in the booth beside her.

She took a moment to imagine the big party that would surely be held in her honor after she exposed these criminals. She thought, *I bet the mayor will be there to present me with a key to the city. Heck, with all of the publicity I will get from this, Oprah will probably catch wind of my heroics and give me some kind of gift as well.*

All the while Sylvia was playing detective, Maggie continued her job as usual, placing and returning with the orders for the two nonlocals. She placed the BLT platter in front of Bradley and the cheeseburger with the mayo on the side in front of Mike. She watched as the men calmly looked at each other then switched the plates to correct Maggie's order mix-up.

Trying to remain professional, she continued on with her job. "Do you need some, umm, ketchup? Or maybe there is something else I can do for you." The older man choked on his drink of tea at the implications of her comment.

She immediately recognized the mistake. "Oh, when I said something, I did not mean something inappropriate. I meant something like getting a refill or a side of dressing. Dear me, not *something!*"

She grabbed the ketchup and mustard from one of the other tables, a handful of napkins, a new set of silverware for each man, a pitcher of tea, and a roll of mints from the register area. She walked over and sat it all on their table. "That should meet every one of your needs!" she said. As she stormed away, their audible snickers caused the temperature of her face to suddenly rise to a very uncomfortable level.

Keeping her eye on Bradley and trying to provide good service for her other patrons was proving to be no easy task, so Maggie was thrilled to see the men pay their bill and leave. The moment the door closed behind them, she slid into an empty booth and pulled back the short red curtain that framed one of the many windows of the diner, wanting to see with her own eyes that the men were truly leaving the parking lot. After seeing the taillights of their vehicle heading down the street, she laid her head back on the soft cushion of the booth, closed her eyes, and took several deep breaths to calm her frazzled nerves. She was jolted back into reality by Mr. Gene's booming voice, "Hey, Sleeping Beauty! Prince Charming called. He's stuck in traffic, so he asked me to wake you."

"Mr. Gene, you are so silly. You know Prince Charming wouldn't be stuck in traffic since he rides a horse. You crack me up! I will go ahead and take my break though." She took his groan as the permission she needed, and before he could change his mind, she plopped down across from Sylvia and began her interrogation.

"Well, what else did you find out? Do you think these men are mobsters? The kind that are related to someone famous, like Jimmy Hoffa? Do you think they have done this kind of thing before? What about their families? Do you think their families know what line of business they are in?"

Sylvia interrupted, "Hold on! One question at a time. I couldn't hear much after you left. I only heard them talking about fishing, and how often they get their oil changed. They are some horribly boring criminals. But before I dozed off from boredom, I did hear the young guy…what was his name? Oh yeah, Bradley, telling the older guy he was staying at the Archers Hotel for a couple of days. What time do you work tomorrow?"

"Why do you ask?" Maggie questioned nervously.

Sylvia replied, "I will need you to pick me up bright and early so we can stake out the hotel."

Maggie shoved back from the table. "No way!"

Sylvia knew how to turn Maggie's no into a yes, and had done it a thousand times. All it took was a little persuasion. Speaking in a very sad and feeble tone, she said, "The life of a defenseless little, petite flower growing in God's garden is in your hands. If your conscience can live with knowing two common thieves want to come and pluck that "flower" from the garden before her time, it is fine by me. Just remember, she is someone's grandmother, just like me." She pulled a hanky from somewhere inside her collar and dabbed at her eyes even though they were completely dry.

Her manipulation tactics in full form, she said, "I thought I knew you, Maggie Mae, but maybe I was wrong."

Maggie's lip began to quiver in sadness. "Okay, I will drive you, but that is all! I refuse to get involved."

Sylvia whispered under her breath, "That's what you think."

"I'm sorry, what did you say?" Maggie asked.

"Oh, I said I think I will wear pink. You know how that color brings out my eyes."

Mr. Gene yelled across the diner, "Hey, princess! Are you going to take these pancakes to table seven, or do you have an ugly stepsister that needs a job?"

Oblivious to his clever insult, she replied, "Pancakes must be served warm. On my way!" She flashed him a warm grin before reaching down and giving Sylvia a hug. "See ya in the morning," she said.

Sylvia wiped her mouth and waited until Maggie was totally focused on the pancake delivery before she slipped her gun back in her purse and headed out the door towards the bus stop.

PLEASE DON'T BE DEAD!

Sylvia got an early start on the day, the excitement of doing private detective work energizing every fiber of her being. Needing her dose of greasy fried eggs, she cooked them quickly before sliding them out of the skillet and onto her plate. She was pulling a chair out to take a seat when she heard a knock on the door. "Who in the world could that be, this early in the morning?" she asked Jake, as if he would actually reply. He raised his eyebrows at the sound of her voice, but that was the extent of his interaction. She gave him a rebuke then stepped over him to make her way to the door. "You are a worthless watch dog. Good thing I don't have a garbage disposal and you eat all my scraps, or I would have no need for you."

She took a quick glance into the mirror that hung beside the front door before answering, taking a moment to tuck in the stray hairs that had escaped overnight from beneath her bright yellow headscarf. She pulled the curtain aside and peeked out. There stood Mr. Newsome, her newspaper in one of his boney, well-manicured hands and a coffee cake in the other.

She unlocked the deadbolt, slid the chain from its base, then turned the knob to complete the unlocking of the door. She pulled it open, and there stood her gentleman caller, smiling ear to ear.

"Good morning, sunshine," he said, so cheerfully it almost came out as a song. "I thought my sweetheart could use a little extra sweetness this morning, so I got up early and baked you my world-famous breakfast confection." He stepped closer and held the cake up to the screen door, enticing her to take a sniff. She closed her eyes as she inhaled deeply, the smell of cinnamon from the still-warm cake filling her nose and lungs.

"Mr. Newsome, you sure know how to charm a girl," she said as she took the cake and newspaper from his hands. "I told you I have sworn off men, but it is sure hard to resist a fella that can bake. You really should get off my porch and stop tormenting me with all of your sexy baking goodness." She held the screen door open as she stepped into his personal space, rose up on her tiptoes, and gently kissed him on the forehead. With that, she stepped back into the house, batted her eyes, and, without saying another word, used her very ample bottom to shut the door behind her.

Holding tightly to her baked gift, she took her elbow and ever so slightly moved the curtain back to check on her "stalker's" location. Her timing was perfect. She watched as Mr. Newsome skipped across the yard then finished off his gleeful dance with a little hop and a click of his heels. She let the curtain drop and headed to the kitchen, smiling with pride. "Jakey Boy, I still got it," she said, holding the cake closer to her face, taking another deep inhale of the intoxicating scent. "Yumm-o! That man sure knows my weakness."

Back at the kitchen table, she could almost hear the recording of her deceased mother's voice playing in her mind, "No dessert until you clean your plate." Sylvia always obeyed that rule, even if the plate she was cleaning was covered in her breakfast.

She began eating her eggs with the same enthusiasm a five-year-old would have when promised candy if he ate his broccoli. After consuming two eggs, a slice of ham, and two biscuits with apple butter, she made herself another cup of instant coffee then sliced off a huge piece of Mr. Newsome's masterpiece covered in sugar and nuts.

She pinched off a hunk, dipped it in her coffee, and popped it in her mouth. A deep moan left her body. "Any man that can cook like this should be married. Maybe I should just surrender to his advances and take him up on his proposal. He may be a bit too skinny for my tastes, but what he lacks in machismo, he sure makes up for in baked goods." She pinched off another piece of the cake and tossed it to Jake who caught the bite in the air and swallowed without even chewing.

"You know, ol' boy, this cake sure is delicious, but sadly, pastries taste so different after they cool off. They are just never as good after they have sat around, and since Mr. Newsome got up before the chickens to make this work of art for me, it would be terribly wrong to let it go bad. Out of consideration for all of his hard work, we should go ahead and cut ourselves another piece."

She took her butcher knife and sliced off another hefty chunk of cake, this time not even wasting any effort by putting it on a plate. She took big bites from the crumble-topped triangle of goodness until it had disappeared. Upon completion, she sat back in her chair and began rubbing her protruding belly.

"Phew! I think I may have overdone it a bit. Now my gut hurts." She walked into the restroom, reached into the medicine cabinet, and pulled out the antacids. Putting two of the chalky tablets in her mouth, she chewed without much attention, washing them down with the last swig of coffee.

She gave Jake a pat on the head then said, "Better do some exercises to get in shape. Now that I'm a crime fighter, I need to make sure my cardiovascular is in good shape. Never know when I will be called upon to run down a bad guy."

She continued talking to her furry roommate, who was now snoring, "As far as police chases go, it will be nice being the 'chaser' and not the 'chasee' this time. Boy, oh boy, I remember the last time I was run down by the cops. Alan, also known as husband number five, got his club raided after someone called in a tip that he was running an illegal cockfighting ring. Even though it wasn't true, when the cops pounded on the door that one fateful night, we thought it best to get out of there quick, just in case there was some legal infraction we may have overlooked. We grabbed our chickens and went into hiding until we had enough information to prove our innocence. No one would ever believe we were raising those birds only for their poop to win some darned contest."

She continued the story, assuming her canine friend wanted to know the details, "Now, buddy, you know I'm a competitive girl, and when I heard there was a contest offering a tour of the ketchup-processing plant to the grower of the largest tomato, I had to win. I pulled out all of the stops. My great-granny always used cow manure to fertilize her garden, and she grew the biggest vegetables in the county, I took a play from her playbook, but since I didn't have enough room behind the tavern for a cow, I improvised and got me some chickens. All was going well in my attempt at a super-garden except for one thing. The neighbor's cat kept sneaking over and killing my feathered "fertilizer makers," so we had to move them into the bar for safety. How was I to know live chickens caged in the back room of a club and dead chickens lying in a dumpster would make people think we were committing a crime."

As she finished her tale, she pulled a pair of Spandex shorts from her dresser drawer, slipped her feet in, and began sliding the stretchy garment up her legs. They went to her knees without much effort, but once they reached her thighs, the opening of the shorts was too small to accommodate the size of the full-figured woman. She continued to try and coax them into place, and with each tug, she became a bit more forceful. "Hmm, guess they must have shrunk," she said breathlessly. "Oh well, once I get them on they will stretch out, and I will be fine."

She pulled and wiggled then jumped up and down a few times, shifting her body enough to force it into the elastic garment. She gave the waistband one last tug and considered it good. Adding a tank top and a colored headband, she had more bumps and rolls than a country road, but she was ready to begin her workout.

She rustled through a pile of books and tapes that were in a wicker basket next to the television until she found a Richard Simmons video she had bought at a garage sale but had never taken out of the package. She took it to the VCR her son had purchased for her as a Christmas gift three years before, which had also never been used. "Now, let's see how this thing works," she said, pushing every button in hopes one of them would give her directions as to what she should do next.

She took her plump finger, pushed open the slot, and peaked inside. She took the tape and tried to slip it in the dark hole, but it just wouldn't go. Not realizing the tape was upside down, she pushed a little harder the second time, hoping a little coaxing was all it needed but still no acceptance.

She took it out, banged it on the side of the TV, and blew on it, knowing these two actions could usually fix most things. She tried again to get it into the slot, but the tape being upside down prevented her success. Not being known for her patience, she walked over and threw the tape into the trash can, stirring Jake from his slumber.

She felt his attention required an explanation. "No one told me these tapes came in different sizes. Of course, I went and bought the large tape when my "CVR" only uses small ones. No big deal really, because I don't need some fuzzy-headed man in shorty-shorts telling me how to move anyway. I know how to work this body." She ran her hands up and down her sides to emphasis her statement.

She stepped into the bedroom and turned on her small transistor radio that was sitting on the nightstand. A quick turn of the volume knob allowed the music to be heard clearly in the front room she had deemed her "work-out gym."

Taking a moment to shove her throw rugs into a pile off to the side, she took her place in the center of the room.

To the beat of the song blaring on the radio, she took a little jump and her feet went hip width while clapping her hands over her head. "One," she said. Jumping again and bringing her hands down to her sides, she brought her feet back together to her beginning stance. She took a moment before attempting another flailing she thought resembled a jumping jack.

"Two," she continued, throwing her limbs around, "three…*owwww!*"

She grabbed the hamstring in her right leg. Putting pressure on the injury, she rubbed it deeply. "The experts say you should listen to your body. I believe mine is saying that muscle has worked enough. Guess it's time to move on to my sit-ups."

She positioned herself close to the couch, using the furniture to steady herself as she went down on her knees, then onto her bottom, finally onto her back, groaning with each transition. Lying on the floor, she told Jake, "First, I must take a deep, cleansing breath. I learned that from the yoga show I always watch while I am trying to take a nap. The music they have on that show puts me to sleep every time." She inhaled deeply, let it out, and began coughing and sputtering. Clearing her throat, she put her hands behind her head and bounced around, trying desperately to lift her upper torso from the ground, but the only parts that lifted were her head and neck.

While she flopped on the floor, looking like a pregnant tuna on dry land, she was unaware Maggie had arrived and was standing on the porch.

Maggie gently knocked on the door, but the volume of Sylvia's workout music drowned out her attempt at getting an answer. She waited a moment before trying again, this time with a little more force. Still no answer.

The third time, motivated by an irrational fear of finding someone dead, Maggie began having a panic attack and her knock represented that adrenalin rush. Pounding on the door, she began to yell, "Sylvia! Open the door! Please, don't be dead!"

She pressed her face against the window and cupped her hands around her eyes trying to focus and look through the curtains. Afraid of what she might find, but knowing she had no choice, she looked inside the house to see if her best friend was in distress. "Sylvia!" Maggie yelled, twisting and yanking on the doorknob. "Open this door and don't you dare be dead! If you are, I am so not coming to you funeral."

The thought of Sylvia in a casket sent Maggie into full-fledged panic mode. "I'm coming in!" she yelled. Stepping off the porch and into the yard, she looked up at the house trying to find a point of entry. The first opening she considered was the chimney.

She swallowed hard and pulled the collar of her blouse, trying to get more air. "Maybe not the chimney. I would probably get stuck in there and die from dehydration. And I refuse to even think about how many spiders live in there." She shuddered. Her stress level was increasing, a little tear spilling over her bottom eyelid and creeping down her cheek. She wiped it on her sleeve. "This is an emergency. I have no choice. I have to save my friend. I will break a window."

While walking to the side of the house to find some type of access, her thoughts were running rampant and tormenting her. *I wonder if she had a heart attack. Nah, a heart attack would be too boring for her. I bet she accidentally shot herself while cleaning her gun. That seems more like Sylvia.*

As she approached the window, she hesitated, not knowing what she was about to find. She stepped close to the house, took a deep breath to calm herself, then put her face up to the window, and looked inside.

"Nooo!" she let out a blood-curdling scream, jumped back and began sobbing hysterically.

The loud commotion brought Mr. Newsome rushing to the scene from his house. "What is wrong, young lady?" he said, his voice shaky from being startled.

"It's Sylvia," she sobbed. "She is dead. I can see her lifeless body lying on the floor. Oh, Mr. Newsome, I warned her to take better care of herself, but she wouldn't listen. And now here we are, left to grieve because she wouldn't put down the salt shaker." She covered her face, the tears now flowing freely.

Mr. Newsome spoke, his words slow and full of sadness. "I just saw her thirty minutes ago, and she looked great. And when I say great, I mean great!" He paused. Maggie looked up, and through her wet eyes, she noticed he was looking off into the distance, grinning.

"Mr. Newsome, control yourself! We are talking about the memory of a good woman. Please, contain your lust and speak kindly about the deceased."

"Oh, sorry, Maggie. I meant no disrespect. I just always had a thing for that woman, and I don't know why she held out on me. And now, I will never know what it would be like to be held tightly in the arms of that love goddess."

His countenance turned sad as he walked up to the window to see for himself the remains of his beloved. He peaked through the glass and once he focused, he began saying in a deep, sultry voice, "Oh, baby, you are so sexy. Mmm, yummy, I tell you. Down right delicious."

Maggie walked up behind him and slapped him on the back of the head. "Ow!" He lifted his hand and put it over the area to sooth the sharp pain. "What in the world did you do that for?"

"You sicko! How dare you ogle my dead friend." Maggie's tears turned to anger.

"Dead? Oh, Maggie. She is far from dead. She is lying on the ground trying to do some kind of exercise. Don't know what kind, but whatever it is, it sure is working. Va-va-voom!"

Maggie shoved him out of the way and looked through the glass, taking longer to get a better view this time. She watched as Sylvia squirmed and strained, trying desperately to lift her shoulders off the ground.

"She is alive! Thank you, God! Oh, I am so glad she is alive!" She began pounding on the window, and this time Sylvia heard the banging over the Slim Whitman song blasting from the radio.

Sylvia slowly looked left, then right, then toward the ceiling, trying to figure out where the pounding was coming from. Another knock from Maggie drew Sylvia's attention to the two silhouettes looking at her through the window. "What in the world…?" she said.

Trying to get into a sitting position was no easy task, but after several grunts and a couple insulting words, she rolled over to her belly, pulled her knees up towards her body, planted her hands on the ground, and began the most difficult task of straightening her legs. With her bottom pointing straight up into the air, she tried to walk her hands towards her feet but stopped, looking like a thick inverted *V*.

"Well, shoot!" She lowered herself back to her hands and knees, then crawled through the living room towards the foyer, before reaching up, and unlocking the door. Maggie and Mr. Newsome, hearing the release of the latch, stepped inside and quickly came to Sylvia's aid.

Standing, one on each side of their kneeling friend, they looped their arms through hers, and counted, "One, two, three!" One good hoist, and Sylvia was again upright and steady. Maggie threw her arms around her friend and began rejoicing. "I am so glad you are not dead! Please, never leave me."

"Now, why in the world would you think I was dead?"

"Well, I uh, you are getting, uh, not so young and, uh..."

Through gritted teeth, Sylvia said very slowly, pronouncing each word distinctly, "Are. You. Saying. That. I. Am. Old?"

Having seen that look on Sylvia's face before, fear once again gripped Maggie, but this time, she thought she was the one who was going to be dead. She looked to Mr. Newsome for help, but his eyes had not left Sylvia's spandex-covered body. He just stood there, hypnotized by her style, a huge smile on his face.

Thankfully, for Maggie's sake, Sylvia also noticed his frozen stare. "Mr. Newsome?" she said, melodically snapping her fingers to bring him out of his trance. He did not respond. She spoke louder the second time, "Mr. Newsome!" The volume of her voice brought him out of his stupor.

"Oh! Sorry, I am just mesmerized by your beauty. I have never seen such a vision of loveliness in my life. It is taking all that I have to keep myself from walking over and burying my face into your ample..."

"Mr. Newsome! We have a young, naive girl here. Why don't you go home and take a cold shower, and I will talk to you later." Giving him a shove to motivate him, she closed the door behind him once he stepped onto the porch. She walked to the bedroom and shut off the radio.

"That man, I swear. He has the hormones of a sixteen-year-old boy."

Maggie was sitting on the couch, bent over with her head between her knees, trying to keep from fainting. Sylvia plopped down in her rocker and pulled a tissue from her sports bra, and began mopping the sweat from her brow.

"Phew! That aerobic stuff is hard work. It is not easy to keep this body sculpted into the work of art that it is." She grinned and nodded her head in pride. "It sure burns a lot of blood sugar, I know that for sure."

She reached into the drawer of her end table and pulled out a candy bar full of nuts and caramel and took a bite. "Want some?" she asked Maggie.

"I think I am going to pass out," Maggie said.

"You are going to pass on it? Okay, then I will have to eat it all myself."

"I didn't say I was going to pass on it. I said I was going to…never mind."

Sylvia, chomping away at the candy, asked, "Are you just going to sit there staring at your belly button, or do you want to hear my plan on how we are going to bring down that scumbag, Bradley?"

Using the candy wrapper to remove the remnants of the snack from between her teeth, she stopped "flossing," and said, "We need to gather information, and there is only one way to do that. We are going to sneak into his hotel room and find out more about the lowlife. I need to go change clothes, then we can get going." Her knees popped and cracked as she headed into the bedroom, not even acknowledging the color had not yet fully returned to Maggie's face.

It took a moment for her words to reach Maggie's hearing since her ears were still roaring from the blood pressure spike caused by her freak out, but once she realized what she had really heard, she knew she had to stop this craziness.

"Sylvia, we need to reconsider. I don't know a lot about the law, but I think that breaking and entering is a crime, and I would prefer to not go to jail. I think we should just call Officer Larry and tell him what we know. He is very capable of handling situations like this. Plus, he can shoot Bradley if he needs to."

Sylvia came busting out of her room in her typical housedress with little collar and three buttons down the front, only this time, she had accessorized it with a big, floppy southern bell hat and dark glasses strategically balanced over her regular eyeglasses. The shades were so large, they covered half of her face, making her look like a giant, cartoon bug.

She was carrying a beach hat with little flip-flops painted on it and an additional pair of sunglasses that she casually tossed to Maggie.

Sylvia said, "First, being a policeman in this town means, Officer Larry has not had to solve a crime bigger than jaywalking in the last fifteen years, so I'm not convinced he is able to bring down an international crime family. Second, everyone in town knows and loves him, so he would never be able to get information like you and I can. I mean, who would ever expect us to be undercover detectives? Just quit being a wimp and get ready."

"Get ready?" Maggie asked.

"We have to conceal our identities. All famous people put on big hats and sunglasses when they want to go out and not be recognized. It works. Just look at me. If you did not know it was me, you would never ever be able to guess who I was."

Sylvia was so recognizable that even if she was wrapped like a mummy, people would still know it was her, but Maggie obliged and took her newly-acquired accessories to the mirror and put them on, adjusting them so very little of her face actually showed. She asked, "Do I really look like a crime fighter? I think I look more like I am heading to the pool."

"Exactly. No one would ever expect a sunbather to be on the trail of two expert criminals, so let's go."

"But it is cold outside, and the pool hasn't even opened yet," Maggie said, self-consciously.

Sylvia had already grabbed her purse and walked out the door, so Maggie had no choice but to follow. Pulling the door shut, she checked to make sure it locked behind her.

THE ART OF PERSUASION OR HARRASMENT–HARD TO TELL THE DIFFERENCE

Maggie drove around to the side of the hotel, pulled the car into a parking spot, and turned the engine off. She and Sylvia watched as the bellman helped a family of five unload their luggage onto the porter's cart.

"Okay, we need to get into that hotel without being noticed. Let me think a minute," Sylvia closed her eyes and leaned her head back onto the headrest.

Maggie didn't have on a watch, but it seemed to her that Sylvia had been lying perfectly still a very long time, and it was creeping her out. She slowly leaned over and got very close to make sure Sylvia was still breathing. Seeing her body rise and fall with each breath was not convincing enough. Maggie reached down and picked up an old, used drinking straw from the floorboard, moved it towards Sylvia's face, and gently poked her in her cheek.

"What the…?"

"Sorry. I was just making sure you were okay," Maggie said, relieved Sylvia was all right.

"Don't poke me when my eyes are closed. You almost made me pee." Sylvia shook her head. "Before I was rudely interrupted, I came up with a plan." She pointed her finger in the direction of the family who was being assisted by the bellman. "We are going to sneak in with them." She pulled down the visor and checked her "disguise."

Maggie was hoping to catch a peak at the handsome Bradley, so she eagerly followed Sylvia's lead, trusting in the wisdom of her elder friend.

The ladies quietly got out of the car and tiptoed to the corner of the building to get a better view of the front door. They watched as the vacationing family stepped into the lobby, leaving the bellman alone with a cart stacked full of suitcases and personal effects. He steadied the items and gave the overstuffed cart a shove. Sylvia and Maggie ran alongside the cart, and stepped in sync, using the suitcases and hanging clothing to keep them well hidden from not only the bellman, but the clerk at the front desk also.

The cart thumped across the ceramic tiles of the hotel foyer as they headed towards the elevator. The crime-fighting team walked beside their "moving shelter" until they reached the housekeeping closet where Sylvia grabbed the door knob, and, in a flash, stepped inside, yanking Maggie by the arm and snatching her into hiding as well.

"What in the world?" Maggie gasped.

"Pay attention!" Sylvia scolded, a bit winded from the excitement.

As she caught her breath, Maggie asked, "What's next?"

"Not sure yet. Give me a second."

"Just don't close our eyes while you think," Maggie pleaded.

Sylvia opened the door a crack, took a peek at the quiet lobby, then lit up when her eyes found what she was looking for. "Perfect!" she said. "I was hoping Sam was working. This will make our job so easy."

Sylvia stepped back inside the closet. "Okay, you are going to the counter where porter Sam is working. Don't worry about him. I have known him since grade school. He was a four-eyed dork who always wore suspenders, and as you are about to see, nothing much has changed. He still wears the same pop-bottle glasses he did in the sixth grade. He has never had a girlfriend, and we are going to capitalize on that need for female companionship. I want you to march out to that counter, "work it," and, just when you have him totally distracted by your womanly charms, ask for Bradley's room number." Sylvia's calm demeanor made this assignment seem completely rational.

"No problem, but I do have one little question first," Maggie said.

"What is it?"

"What are womanly charms, and how exactly do I work them?"

"Think Mae West or maybe Jane Russell."

"Who?" Maggie asked, a puzzled look on her face.

"Oh, sorry. Generation gap. Think Angelina Jolie. With just a look, she can have a man crawl across broken glass to mop sweat off of her upper lip. All you have to do is muster up all of your estrogen, think seductress, and get that room number. Now, go use what the good Lord gave ya." Sylvia looked her friend up and down, then clarified, "Well, at least do the best you can."

"I'm a seductress. Seduct—ress. Su-duck-rest. That is a funny word." Maggie giggled.

"Go!" Sylvia said, firmly.

"I am glad you believe in me. If you think I can, I think I can." She took off her beach hat but left on the sunglasses. "I think these make me look mysterious."

She went to open the closet door, but Sylvia grabbed her hand. "Hold on." She reached up and unbuttoned the top button of Maggie's shirt. "There, that is better. Remember, seductress."

Maggie opened the door and stepped out. Her confidence was short-lived, as she saw porter Sam standing behind the counter shuffling through some papers. The magnitude of the task she had been given suddenly hit her, causing such an adrenaline rush that her body went weak. She wanted to run back to the safety of the closet, but her legs were so wiggly, all she could do was stand in place and wobble.

Sylvia, watching her plan unfold through a crack in the door, immediately knew something had gone wrong.

She whispered loud enough that Maggie could hear every word. "Focus! This task would be nothing for Angelina Jolie, and you are working with the all the same equipment she has, so go!"

Maggie nodded in agreement, took a deep breath, and began walking towards the desk. In her mind, her walk was captivating and sexy, but in actuality, she looked as if she was lame in one leg. With her hand on her hip, she put one foot forward then dragged her other foot up to meet it, hoping to appear irresistible as she made her way towards the unsuspecting man.

Arriving at the counter, she leaned onto it, and took her index and middle finger and walked them across the flat surface towards Sam. He was so deeply involved in his work, he never even noticed her.

Becoming more persistent, she leaned deeper onto the counter, reached up and removed her ponytail holder and shook her head to tousle her hair. Once again, Sam never looked up.

She began flipping her head even harder, trying desperately to get his attention. Dizziness was an immediate by-product of the excessive hair-whipping. She laid her face on the cool marble of the counter. "Excuse me, I think I am going to be sick," she said.

This cry for help finally got Sam's attention. "Are you okay?" he asked, in a very feeble but compassionate voice.

The room had stopped spinning, but Maggie took a moment to refocus on her task. She thought, *Sexiness, it is. I am a beast. This man is putty in my hands.* She lifted her head, began batting her eyes, and slowly licked her lips as she leaned deeper towards Sam.

He looked at her with a very puzzled expression, lifting his small, round, wire-framed eyeglasses higher onto his nose to get a better look.

"Ma'am, do you have a medical condition?"

"No, sir, I am just fine. But not as fine as you, big fella."

"Excuse me?" Sam asked, backing up and nervously adjusted his bow tie. He took his arms and self-consciously crossed them to cover himself as if he had just been caught coming out of the shower.

Maggie felt the tension, which quickly turned to embarrassment. She stood up and buttoned her top button. She felt hot, and it was not the sexy kind of hot. It was the humiliated kind.

Sylvia had been watching her protégé floundering and said to herself, "You can't send a girl to do a woman's job."

She took her hands and placed her ample breasts in a perkier position, but the moment she let them go, gravity put them back where they normally hung. Shrugging it off, she fluffed her hair before strutting over to the counter. Her arrival brought Maggie back from the "land of humiliation."

Not saying a word, Sylvia pointed towards the closet from which she had come, and Maggie responded like a five-year-old who was just sent to time out. Sam was terribly confused, and Sylvia's arrival only made it worse.

"So, young man, what brings you to a place like this?" Sylvia asked.

Sam adjusted his glasses again. "Miss Sylvia, you do know I work here, right? It's me, Sam. We went to school together, and you gave me my first kiss behind the roller skating rink. Don't you remember?"

"Oh, Sammy, I could never forget that kiss," she lied. "I have thought about it over and over, and over." She began fanning herself as she tried to convince him of the affect the kiss had on her.

"Really?" he asked. "Then explain to me why I have seen you out and about at least a hundred times since then, and you never even acknowledge me. Well, except for the time you saw me at a baseball game, and you threw your hot dog at me."

She looked at him, winked, and blew him a kiss before continuing her lie. "I saw you every one of those times, but I would not allow myself to speak to you because I could not stand another heartbreak. And the hot dog incident? Well, that was like a love tap. I am sure you just misunderstood. I would have never barked at someone as handsome as you.

Sam looked deep into Sylvia's eyes, hoping for some kind of explanation as to why the women were acting so oddly. "I think there may be a gas leak in the hotel," he informed Sylvia.

"What?" she squealed.

He began walking around, sniffing the air, trying to find the source of the leak. He blurted out, "Miss Sylvia, I think you and your friend may need an ambulance. Please lay down while I call for help."

"I don't need an ambulance, you crazy…I mean, I don't need an ambulance, but I could sure use a little mouth-to-mouth," Sylvia said, running her finger down her neck towards her chest.

"Sylvia! What is wrong with you?"

She could not put up with the charade any longer. Reaching across the counter, she grabbed Sam by the collar, crushing his perfectly tied bow tie.

"Here's the deal, Bucko. Since we are obviously getting nowhere fast, let's cut to the chase. You have something I want, and I will get it one way or another," she snarled.

Sweat began to form on his forehead and he swallowed hard. She continued, "Here is what I need. There is a man staying in this flea-infested hotel. He checked-in yesterday, and he is one of them "big city folks." He was wearing a fancy suit and some very shiny shoes. He goes by the name, Bradley. I need to know which room he is staying in. Now, you can freely give me that information and life will go well with you or"—she paused for dramatic effect—"or you can hold out, which means I have no choice but to wrestle you to the ground, sit on you, and use the tweezers I have in my purse to pluck every single hair off of your body."

Her nostrils were flaring, her teeth clenched shut, her lips never moving as the words hissed from her mouth. Sam, when given the new option, wished he would have gone with Sylvia's first proposition, as unpleasant as it seemed.

She let go of his collar and gently took her hands and smoothed his wrinkled shirt. She smiled at him, not demurely this time. More like the grin a cartoon lion would make right before it devoured its prey.

He shuddered. The wrath of his boss would be nothing compared to the torture this large, angry woman was about to put him through.

He walked over to the registry and ran his finger down the page, then across, then stopped. He took a small scrap of paper and wrote a number on it, sliding it across the counter to her. She looked at it and smiled, her eyelashes fluttering. She slid the paper back across the counter. "And the full name of that gentleman would be?"

He rolled his eyes and sighed heavily. He took the paper back over to the registry, scribbled the name above the room number, and handed it back to his blackmailer.

"Sam, you have always been my favorite clerk," she said, as she looked down at the information.

"Yeah, right. I'm not your favorite. I'm just the only one you can beat up!"

She stopped grinning and said, "Good point." She turned and walked towards the front door.

Maggie, peeking out of the closet, saw Sylvia motion for her to follow. Shuffling to catch up, she heard Sylvia proclaim, "Now that is how you use your womanly charms."

"You didn't tell me that choking the man counted as charms," Maggie said.

"I wasn't choking him. I was pulling him closer. I wanted him to feel my breath on his skin. And what does it matter anyway? The point is I have the information that I came for. That is victory, baby. Sweet victory. And speaking of sweet, my blood sugar is dropping and that makes me grouchy. So unless you want to see me get really fussy, we should probably go get some pie."

Not wanting another scene, Maggie asked her, "How about The Spot?"

BREAKING AND ENTERING FOR THE GOOD OF OTHERS

MORNING SEEMED TO come extra early, but Maggie wouldn't miss work even though her heart and mind were far away from serving customers. There were already enough distractions, and it didn't help that Sylvia had called the diner four times that day, each time with a new idea on how to get information about Bradley. Knowing Mr. Gene was not a big fan of Sylvia only added to her stress, putting pressure on Maggie to make up a different story each time she called.

Now that her shift was over, she smiled proudly at her ability to think so quickly on her feet. From telling Mr. Gene the "callers" were a person selling insurance, a Japanese-speaking lady that called a wrong number, a recorded message regarding the upcoming vote, and a not-for-profit organization that wanted donations to help save abused animals, she felt her lying was proof she was really tapping into her inner private detective.

Turning onto Sylvia's street, she could see her friend on the front porch, pacing back and forth like a gorilla at the zoo. Sylvia, hearing the vehicle approaching, sprinted out to the sidewalk, barely allowing the car to come to a stop before opening the door.

"I thought you were never going to get here!" she snapped.

"I know, right? It was so hard to focus at work today. All I could do was wonder what in the world we are going to find in that hotel room. What if we come across something really scary like weapons or a bomb or, even worse, women's underwear?"

"Funny tidbit," Sylvia said, as she climbed into the car and buckled her seat belt. "My sixth husband was an accountant who liked wearing women's underwear. He had the nicest selection of undergarments I had ever seen. Those fancy frillies were the reason our marriage ended. Not because he wore them but because he wouldn't share. I still remember the big fight that ended it all. It was a Thursday, which was laundry day. I was going to do the wash, so I had put all of my undies in the clothes basket to be cleaned. Since I wasn't a fan of going commando, I didn't think he would mind if I borrowed a pair from his collection. Boy was I wrong. When he came home and found out that I was wearing a pair of his black, satin bikinis, he got so angry that he sat down on the couch and cried. He kept accusing me of "desecrating the collection." After he whimpered and whined for about a week, I packed up and left. I could handle a man that wore women's clothes, but I was not going to be married to a cry baby."

Maggie kept her eyes on the road and tried desperately to keep from giggling. Sylvia changed the subject. "All of this crime fighting is causing my metabolism to race. I am just emaciated. I need you to run me by the bread store before we go to the hotel. I am completely out of bread, and I could really use a little snack before we get too far into this thing."

"You got it, boss." Maggie said, making the tires squeal as she made a sudden, unplanned left turn.

After a quick jaunt through the store, Sylvia paid for a loaf of Home Pride bread, three boxes of chocolate cupcakes with little white swirls on top, an angel food cake, and six fried, fruit pies.

The drive from the bakery to the hotel was a short one with an excited Maggie behind the wheel. Agreeing the back entrance was the most inconspicuous, they found a spot at the farthest end of the lot and parked the vehicle.

While Maggie quieted herself to contemplate what to do next, Sylvia was already outside of the car, doing a hamstring stretch. She completed her warm up with a lunge then said, "Let's go." Maggie watched as Sylvia sprinted towards the building, where she quickly flattened herself against the wall before sliding behind a well-manicured evergreen bush. She was about three foot taller and two foot wider than the bush she was hiding behind but was oblivious to the size differential. She quickly looked left and right for a safe route.

Maggie chose a different technique. She walked over, took hold of the door knob, and pulled it open, allowing easy access through the side door of the building. She strolled to the elevator, totally unnoticed. The doors opened, and she stepped inside, pressing the number three when Sylvia jumped in beside her.

"Where in the world did you go?" Maggie asked with a puzzled look. Sylvia, never breaking character, remaining intense and stoic.

Maggie raised her eyebrows and shrugged her shoulders as the doors closed and the elevator rose, coming to a stop on the third floor.

The doors opened, and Sylvia peaked out, taking her arm to hold Maggie back until announcing, "Okay, the coast is clear." She stepped off the elevator, Maggie following close behind, as they headed towards the room reserved by Bradley.

Creeping slowly around the corner, Sylvia said in a hushed voice, "Bingo."

Maggie looked over Sylvia's shoulder and saw the cleaning lady's cart parked down the hall from Bradley's room. She listened while Sylvia explained. "We will wait until she opens his door, then we will have to act fast. I am going to climb underneath that cart and wait there until the cleaning woman pushes me into the room. I'll hide out there until she leaves."

"Okay, what do you want me to do?" Maggie asked, her eyes wide with excitement.

Sylvia watched as the maid pulled the door shut on the previous room then lifted her ring of keys to open the room they knew was Bradley's. The moment the domestic stepped inside, Sylvia said, "Watch my skills." She stepped around the corner where the cart was left unattended, skipped down the hallway, and, when she reached the cart, turned around and pointed to the side of her head, mouthing to Maggie, "I am so smart."

Pulling back the curtain that covered the bottom shelf of the cart, she proceeded to squeeze her plus-sized body into a slim-sized cavity.

Hearing the clanging of the keys carried by the housekeeper getting louder as she was getting closer, she refused to abort the mission. Committing fully to her plan, she quickly shoved herself into the small area. The tight fit caused her forward motion to come to an abrupt stop; her head, neck, and shoulders swallowed up by fluffy white towels while the rest of her body struggled to burrow deeper into the pile. Moving her arms and legs like a frog swimming upstream, each shove she made caused the cart to tip a little more time, until it eventually leaned so far, it could not be righted. As in slow motion, tiny bottles of shampoo and conditioner began flying in the air, along with shower caps and shoe-shining clothes. Sylvia popped out and landed on her bottom, just in time to watch the cart and all of its contents crash in front of her.

Bang! Clang! Crash! The housekeeper, a dark-haired and very husky woman with a very obvious mustache, began yelling, "Look what you did, you crazy woman! You will clean up that mess. I clean up after guests, not after crazy old ladies!"

Not about to blow her cover, Sylvia crawled over to the cart and took hold of it, acting as if she was so old and feeble she was unable to get to her feet.

"Honey, won't you please help me up? I am an old woman. I can barely see, and I cannot figure out who in the world would have parked this cart in the walkway."

The housekeeper raised one eyebrow, crossed her arms, and began tapping her foot. "Oh, my mistake. I did not realize your vision was impaired. Let me gather up my stuff and get it out of your way. I just need you to hold my keys." She yanked the key ring from the clip that held them securely to her belt and threw them to Sylvia, who was now standing upright. Sylvia snatched the keys out of the air with one hand like a professional first baseman. In that instant, she knew she was busted.

The housekeeper began chastising Sylvia as if she was a seven-year-old that refused to pick up her toys. "You are picking up every single item and putting them back exactly like they were."

Sylvia stepped up close to the face of the domestic helper and said, "Now, listen here, you rude old cuss. Haven't you ever heard of something called an accident?"

Maggie watched as the conversation between Sylvia and the cleaning lady began to escalate. As Sylvia began listing the reasons why she was "not about to clean up that mess," she kept sliding slowly around the housekeeper until she had strategically placed herself between the irate hotel employee and Maggie.

Once in place, she took her hand behind her back and discreetly pointed towards the door, indicating to Maggie it was time to make a move.

At the perfect moment, Sylvia reached up and threw her arms around the neck of the housekeeper. "Honey, I'm so sorry. I do not know what in the world came over me. Please forgive me," she said, watching out of the corner of her eye as Maggie slipped behind the housekeeper who was unable to see a thing with the choke hold she was in.

The lady did not appreciate the unwanted physical contact and tried to break free, but Sylvia held on tightly, keeping her eye on Maggie until she was safely in Bradley's hotel room. The second she disappeared, Sylvia released her grip on the now-sweaty and uncomfortable maid.

Sylvia straightened her glasses which had been jostled in the "hugging" and said, "I have these new bifocals and still cannot see a thing. As a matter of fact, I see two of you right now, but that is a pleasure because you are such a doll, that is twice as much goodness. I bet you are your dear, sweet mama's favorite child. How could one not love that adorable face?" Sylvia stepped close again and squeezed the cheeks of the very confused woman tightly between her hands, smooshing her face until she had fish lips. "You have been more than kind, but I must be going now. My granddaughter is going to pick me up and take me for ice cream."

Before walking away, she once again grabbed hold of the poor unsuspecting housekeeper, but this time she squeezed her so tightly, her eyes appeared to slightly bug out.

Kissing the cleaning lady on the forehead before she released her, she said, "Okay, I have to go now. Love ya, darlin'. Keep up the good work." She turned and walked spryly to the elevator, leaving the woman dazed and confused.

Maggie was in a panic and immediately regretted her decision the moment she crossed the threshold into the room. Knowing it was "game on," she ran across the hotel room, dove onto the bed, and rolled until she ran out of mattress, landing with a thud between the bed and the wall. She scooted back towards the bed, trying to get as close as possible, then laid there, awaiting Sylvia's rescue.

The hotel room door was still open, and Maggie listened as the housekeeper picked up the mess from the Sylvia-induced explosion. She held her breath as she heard the door close and lock. The room seemed eerily quiet which only magnified the sound of Maggie's heart pounding in her chest. She reached up and placed two fingers on the side of her neck, checking her pulse, "Please, God, don't let me have a heart attack in this room," she whispered.

Her eyes widened as she heard a faint knock on the door. She closed her eyes tightly and made a wish, "When I open my eyes, I will be tucked safely in my bed."

She popped her eyelids open and found she was in the same location. "Shoot," she said.

She heard another knock, and this one was a little bit louder. Slowly, she got up and moved towards the door, preparing her defense in her mind. *If this is not Sylvia, I will act like I have amnesia. I will tell them I'm lost and do not know who I am.* Dreading what was on the other side of the door, Maggie slowly stood tall and put her eye up to the peep hole. To her relief, it was Sylvia. She flung open the door and threw her arms around the neck of her friend.

"Oh, my goodness! I feel like a superhero! You should have seen me. I was like a ninja. I snuck in here, did a tuck-and-roll over the bed, and then—"

"That's great, but we need to get a move on it. That crazy housekeeper just went down the hall to straighten her cart, so we don't know how much time we have. We can relive our heroics later."

Sylvia walked over to the tweed suitcase that was lying neatly on the luggage rack, put it onto the bed, flipped the latch, and it popped open.

She ransacked through the items of the suitcase without any hesitation while Maggie watched on. "Oh, he's a boxer, not a briefs kind of guy," she said, tossing a pair of the man's undergarment towards Maggie, causing the young girl to blush then pray a short prayer of forgiveness.

Sylvia exclaimed, "Ah ha!" She held up a small box of pseudoephedrine. "He also makes meth."

"What in the world are you talking about?" Maggie replied.

"Methamphetamines," Sylvia explained. "I saw a report on CNN that drug dealers cook these seemingly harmless antihistamines, and it turns into drugs, and they sell it to little children. What a disgusting pig!"

Sylvia left the suitcase open and walked over and picked up a suit jacket which was hanging over the back of a chair. Her pudgy fingers pulled out a folded, yellow piece of paper from inside the pocket. As her eyes focused on the print, she gasped, "Oh, my goodness! Look at this. Wow, Maggie, this is worse than we thought."

Maggie moved closer to take a look at the piece of paper Sylvia was holding. "What is it?" she asked.

"It is a receipt from a company called Big Bang Explosion Factory. This lousy punk is planning on blowing the old bag to smithereens! I guess that will make disposing of her body a lot easier." She looked closely at the receipt. "This shows they have bought so much firepower, they are only going to need a squeegee and a shovel to clean up her remains."

The ladies stopped their conversation and listened as the sound of men's voices began getting closer to the room.

Sylvia shoved and smashed Bradley's clothes back in the suitcase and closed it before grabbing Maggie's hand and pulling her over to the balcony door. She unlocked the latch, slid opened the door, and pulled Maggie outside, slamming the door behind them.

Standing there, silently listening through the glass as the men entered the room, they immediately recognized Bradley's now familiar voice. "I will meet you for dinner in the lounge. I can't wait for this weekend. We are so freaking brilliant, and soon enough, everyone will know how ruthless we are."

After a moment of shared laughter, the door was shut, and the room got quiet. Sylvia leaned around and peeked through a thin slit in the curtain, watching as Bradley picked up the TV remote and turned on ESPN.

"Sy-Sy-Sylvia, I think this is a bad time to tell you, bu-bu-but I have a terrible fear of h-h-heights."

Sylvia never looked towards Maggie but offered some advice as she continued the surveillance. "Well, just look straight down. That should help."

Taking her mentor's advice, she slid her feet slowly to the rail and looked over.

"Sylvia, help," she said in a weak, squeaky voice.

Sylvia turned and saw Maggie, frozen in place, shaking like a leaf.

"What in the world are you doing over by the railing? Get over here!"

"You told me t-t-to look down, and now I can't move."

"Hmm, maybe I got confused. Maybe they say, don't look down. Let's try this. Look straight up and walk towards the sound of my voice."

"Oh, okay." She looked straight into the sky as Sylvia coached her back off the ledge. "Closer. Closer. You are almost here." Maggie's last step was a lunge, plastering herself flat against the wall with her arms spread out, giving the appearance of a bug splattered on the windshield of a fast-moving car.

With Maggie safely back in place, Sylvia watched as Bradley headed to the bathroom.

She pressed her ear against the sliding glass door until she heard the shower start up. With absolute finesse, she slid the door open so slowly, not a sound was made. Without hesitation, she began tiptoeing towards the exit.

Maggie looked like an amoeba, slithering her body across the wall before slipping around the corner of the doorway and into the room. A deep breath with a slow exhale helped calm her nerves until she realized there was a naked man in the shower just feet away from her. That thought made her want to run. She slammed the sliding door closed, catching the curtain on the handle, and the repercussions were immediate.

The curtain rod hit the door, then the desk, and then the end table before it came to a rest on the ground; each time it connected with an item, the noise of the crash got louder. The unexpected clamor sent a shock through Sylvia who wasted no time saving herself, her high-stepping moves allowing her to get out the door before her clumsy accomplice even knew what had just happened.

Maggie grabbed the pile of metal and fabric and began shoving them atop the doorway in hopes it would magically rehang itself, but the sound of the shower shutting off stopped her redecorating. She opened the patio door and threw the curtains onto the balcony before running out of the room, pulling the door shut behind her. The adrenaline gave her supernatural speed, so it didn't take her long to reach the elevator where Sylvia was waiting very impatiently.

"In the elevator, kid!" Sylvia said.

The doors closed with the ladies inside, neither one saying a word, as Sylvia was still trying to catch her breath from the sprint down the hall, and Maggie was hyperventilating. They never looked back until they were looking at the hotel from the rearview mirror of Maggie's car.

SEXY CAN BE PURCHASED AT THE MALL

MAGGIE COULD HEAR the gentle tapping of the rain as it fell on the roof. Her eyelids refused to open, as she was still tired from staying awake late into the night, thinking about Bradley. Even though it was her day off, there was going to be no time to rest. If she was going to get him to divulge his secret life to her, she was going to have to up her game. Today's "not so free" time was going to be filled with a trip to the mall to stock up on the items that she was convinced were needed to help her break down all of his defenses.

Thunder crashing from a spring storm kept her tension high. "Crazy, Midwest weather. I sure hope we don't have a tornado." Before stepping in the shower, she cleared a path to the basement just in case the weather sirens went off, providing her with an easier route to shelter if disaster struck. *Darn you, Dorothy and Toto,* she thought. *I wasn't scared of storms till I saw that stupid show.* Getting dressed in a rush, the next ten minutes were spent searching for her umbrella. Not under the bed, not in the hallway closet, not under the kitchen sink, nor in the basement, she finally located it behind the couch.

Stepping into the kitchen, she found her father sitting at the table with a cup of coffee and a bacon-and-egg sandwich. "Well, aren't you up bright and early?" he said.

"Yes, I have several errands to get done today."

"Be careful out there. The roads will be slick because of the rain, and I don't want to get a call from Officer Larry informing me that you slid into a retaining wall."

"I'll be careful, Daddy. I love you."

"I love you too, honey. Lock the door on your way out because I need to get into the shower."

"Okay. I'll see you later tonight." She gave his shoulder a squeeze and headed out the door, pulling it closed tightly behind her, twisting the knob back and forth to make sure it had locked. She stood on the porch momentarily, hoping for a brief break in the rain.

No such luck. She pushed the button on the handle of the umbrella causing it to spring open. "Well, doggone it." One half of the umbrella was standing straight out, the other half was drooping and flapping in the wind. Strategically placing her tiny frame under the part that was horizontal, she sprinted across the driveway, grabbed the door handle of her car, and gave it a yank. It snapped back without effect. It was locked.

She took her purse from her shoulder and replaced the strap's location with the handle of the umbrella, holding it securely with her chin while she rummaged through her handbag, trying desperately to find her keys.

The wind had picked up, blowing the precipitation under the umbrella and into her eyes, making the "treasure hunt" for her keys even more difficult. Her hands, now soaking wet, had difficulties holding on to the purse, and it began to slip. Lunging for the handbag released the pressure being held on the umbrella, but an impulse squeeze of her shoulder steadied it. Her relief was followed by regret, as the purse flipped upside down, spilling all of the contents into a giant puddle. A sudden gust turned the umbrella wrong side out, giving no protection to the ever-increasing rain.

"Fiddlesticks!" she exclaimed. She dropped the umbrella and watched as it blew across the yard, before bending down and scooping up the mud soaked items, and shoving them back into the drenched bag. "Well, at least now I am sure the keys are not in my purse." She stood up, water dripping from her nose and eyelashes, and headed back to the house.

All it took was a firm hold on the doorknob to remind her that the house, not unlike the car, was also locked. She pounded on the door, hoping her father would rescue her. He soon answered, wrapped in his robe, his hair sudsy and sticking every which direction.

"What in the world? Get in this house! What are you thinking? Don't you know you can catch pneumonia in weather like this?" He ran to the bathroom, grabbed a towel, then returned to Maggie and began blotting her hair and face.

"Young lady, you need to be more careful. You remember what happened to Mr. James when he was in the community theater production of *Moby Dick*? There was that scene where they sprayed him with a garden hose, pretending it was whale spit, and after five shows and one matinee, he came down with the pneumonia and was dead in three days. You need to go put on some dry clothes right now!"

"Sorry, Daddy. I lost my keys somewhere, but I'll go change before I look for them." She ran to her room, pulled off her soaking wet clothes, and threw them in the general vicinity of the clothes hamper. Taking a dry pair of jeans and t-shirt from the pile on the floor, she slipped them on and topped off her ensemble with a gray hoodie with a big stain on the left shoulder.

Her search for the keys ended after she examined the jacket she had worn the night before. The keys were right where she left them—in the pocket.

Her father, shampoo still in his hair, was waiting by the door when she came downstairs with a scarf, a rain hat, mittens, a cup of hot tea, and two vitamin C capsules in his hands. "Here, you'll need these."

Before she could even speak, her father pulled the hat down over her head, wrapped the scarf around her neck, and flicked the end over her shoulder. He handed her the other items then gave her a hug. "Now, be careful this time. You and I both know that 77 percent of all car accidents happen within fifteen minutes from the home."

"I will make sure I buckle up." She walked out the door, waving at her father before running through the rain to her car.

With no more delays, she soon arrived at the local mall where she made a beeline for the cosmetics counter. Standing in the midst of racks full of lotions, creams, makeup, and perfumes, she was overwhelmed at her choices. Reaching up and taking hold of a random tube, she began reading the package in hopes the label would give her a clue as to what it was, and how it was to be applied.

Must be lipstick, she thought. Stepping in front of an acrylic-trimmed mirror strategically placed on the glass counter, she puckered up and dragged the mystery makeup across her lips. Her mistake was immediately apparent as her lips became the same color as her skin, causing them to seemingly disappear.

Maggie heard a woman giggle before speaking in a sweet southern drawl. "That is our Magic Wand concealer. It helps hide blemishes and those nasty dark circles some women get below their eyes. It is a versatile product and can be used for a lot of things, but I have never seen it applied as a lipstick before."

Maggie turned and saw a young lady behind her, wearing a white lab coat with the name "Doty" embroidered slightly below her right shoulder. "Maybe I can help you."

Her bleached-blonde hair was teased and sprayed then teased again, making it stand six inches high on top of her head. A heavy coat of blue glitter had been swiped across her eyelids, and the set of extra-long false eyelashes made her appear as if spiders had taken up residence on her face. Maggie knew at that moment she had found her expert.

She asked quietly, "I am looking for lipstick but not just any lipstick. I would like something, um, sexy."

"Darlin', I know exactly what you need. Let's see, with your skin coloring, I would suggest Red Hot Vixen. It is a true red, so it will make your teeth look whiter, and the bonus is it tastes like cinnamon, which drives the men wild." The Southern belle shuffled through a display case and pulled out a tube. "Here you go, darlin'. Now my name, as you can see, is Doty," she said while pointing to her embroidered name tag. "I will be your makeup consultant today. First, we should talk about getting some blush on those cheeks to emphasize your high cheekbones, and, girl, you desperately need a couple coats of mascara." She took Maggie by the hand and led her to a pink leather and chrome chair.

"Have a seat right here and we can get started with your courtesy Spring Re-birth Makeover." She gave the seat of the chair a pat to direct Maggie's placement.

"Oh, I'm sorry. I can't stay but thanks for the offer. I am in a huge hurry. I have several other errands to run before I—"

"Now, now," she interrupted, "don't tell me you do not have the time to become beautiful. I can show you how to look as gorgeous as me in three minutes flat." She turned and looked at her own reflection in the mirror, smiling at what she saw.

Maggie compared her reflection with the consultant's and knew there was not enough makeup in the building to make them look similar. She humbly said, "There is no way in the world I can look as beautiful as you."

"You just sit back and let me show you how easy it is."

Not wanting to hurt the feelings of the glittery gal, Maggie sat down in the pink chair and let the self-proclaimed artist begin. It was a blur of brushes, liquids, and powders; and three minutes later, just as she predicted, Maggie was spun around to see her reflection in the mirror.

"Oh, my!" she exclaimed.

"Darlin', you could enter a beauty pageant! With your high cheekbones and that elegant neck of yours, you could join *America's Next Top Model.*" Maggie leaned forward to get a closer look in the mirror. She did not see the reflection of a top model. More like a Dolly Parton impersonator whose makeup had been applied with a paint gun.

While posing in the mirror trying to process what she was seeing, she could hear *beep, beep, beep, beep, beep* coming from the area where the cash register was located.

The noise stopped, and Doty announced, "Okay. With the cleanser and bonus astringent, that will be $212.72."

Maggie began looking around to see if there was another customer close at hand who perhaps Doty was talking to, but she quickly realized she was the only one at the counter, and that total was the amount she was expected to pay for the instruments of beauty she was being sold.

Dotty looked at Maggie like a proud mother looks at her child. She was giddy with excitement, her hands clasped under her chin, her shoulders pulled up close to her ears. Once Maggie saw the huge smile on her face, she knew denying the purchase would insult the "artist" and, more importantly, it would break her heart, and Maggie just couldn't do that.

She took her wallet from her purse and did a quick count of her money. "Maybe I should just take the lipstick," Maggie said.

"Don't you like your makeup? Didn't I do a good job? My husband told me I would never make it as a makeup consultant. He said I was better suited as a convenient store clerk. I guess he was right." Her eyes began to fill with tears.

"No, no, that is not it at all. What I was going to say was, I will take the lipstick in a different bag. I just wanted to keep it separate so I wouldn't have to dig for it in case I need to reapply it. I believe you are a true artist. I cannot remember ever looking this beautiful." Maggie secretly crossed her fingers and asked for forgiveness under her breath for the whopper of the lie she just told.

"Really?" she took a tissue from a box next to the mirror and blotted her eyes, careful to not smear her makeup. "I am so glad you can see it too, because from where I am standing, I think you look like a younger, skinnier Cindy Crawford. Well, minus the mole."

"Oh, I agree. And it is all thanks to you and your brilliance." Maggie framed her face with her hands. "You brought this butterfly out of her cocoon. My life will never be the same. Now let's get this paid for so I can go show my new face to the world."

Maggie, ignoring the feelings of buyer's remorse, pulled out her credit card and handed it to Doty, who swiped the card, and while waiting for it to process, explained how the eye shadow could go from daytime to evening. "Now, just use a little of the dark shadow around the lash line, creating what we call the 'smoky eye.' Men find that sultry look irresistible!"

Maggie was trying hard to concentrate, despite the intense burning and itching she was beginning to feel on her neck and ears. Doty handed her the credit card, receipt, and a pretty, pink bag full of the items Maggie doubted would ever be used again.

Once the transaction was complete, Doty came around the counter and gave Maggie a hug. "Thank you so much for your purchase. I am thrilled that you got to be my first sale. I can go home tonight and tell my husband he was wrong. I knew I was destined to be a makeup artist."

Maggie returned the hug then said, "You are going to go far in this business. Keep your dream alive. Thanks for your help." Taking hold of the bag, she headed out the door, scratching her nose, then her ears, then her hairline.

Are my eyes beginning to swell? she wondered, trying to catch a glimpse of her reflection in the window before entering the store that used models in wings to sell bras, panties, and other unmentionables.

Giving herself a pep talk before walking in, she thought, *Okay, just because I have never been able to even look at the mannequins in the windows without blushing, does not mean I do not have as much right as anyone else to march into that store and make a purchase. I am not doing this for me anyway. It is for a sweet, little lady who is about to be ambushed by her punk of a grandson.*

Rubbing her itchy eyes as she entered, she stopped for a moment to clear her vision. Once everything came into focus, she scanned the room full of foundational garments. "Wow, I didn't realize brassieres and panties came in that many colors!"

She walked past the first rack where the bras made with animal-print material hung. "Don't think that is exactly what I am looking for, but then I'm not sure what type of bra a girl needs to trap a man."

As the sales clerk approached, Maggie was slightly stunned and admittedly impressed at how the size-two clerk with the double Ds stood straight upright, not being pulled forward by the odd distribution of weight.

"I need a brassiere that can make me, well…look like you," Maggie said, as she pointed at the buxomly girl.

"That is easy. I am wearing the Sex Kitten Push-Up bra. We can get you in one of these right away. Follow me."

Upon hearing the description of the brassiere, Maggie knew she was in uncharted territory, and it was making her very uncomfortable. To go from the matronly-style undergarments she ordinarily wore, to the Sex Kitten Push-Up, seemed like a very long jump.

Once they arrived at the specific, round table full of bras in difference shapes and colors, the clerk took the tape measure that hung around her neck and reached around Maggie's back as if she was going to give her a big hug. Pulling the tape around, she held it tightly between Maggie's breasts.

Maggie felt her breath become shallow from the personal space invasion, and just when she thought she should slap the clerk for touching her inappropriately, the busty helper said, "You are a 34B." Maggie uncomfortably looked around to make sure no one was watching while the young lady dug through the pile of lace and padding to find just the right size.

The store was filled with sexy mannequins dressed in only their underwear, whose eyes looked sleepy and seductive. She studied the plastic women, thinking, *In all my life, that look has never crossed my face.*

Closing her eyes halfway and puckering her lips, she put her hand on her hip and thrust the lower half of her body forward in an attempt to look "sexy," just like the plastic model. Her acting lesson was interrupted by the salesclerk.

"Here we are. We have your size in Vixen Black, Golden Globes, and Virginal White."

Maggie reached out and grabbed the white one without hesitation, the description alone making the decision for her. Not wanting any questions asked, she handed her credit card to the clerk and said with all the confidence she could muster, "Lovely choice."

Stepping out of the store after the purchase was complete, she squeezed the air out of the bag that contained her newly purchased bra, flattened it, and tucked it under her shirt before leaving the mall. *This crime fighting is not only expensive, it's embarrassing*, she thought.

Scurrying across the parking lot to her car, she threw the bags into the passenger seat before taking her place behind the wheel. Pulling the list of "things to do" she had written on a small piece of yellow paper from her pocket, she took a pen from the storage area on the inside of the door and marked through the words *lipstick* and *bolder holder*. The last item on the list to be completed said "lessons in love."

"One more stop before I am done. I need to know how a woman can romance a man and get him to do anything they want, and there is only one way to get that type of expert information—the movies." A brief stop at the video store would provide her with an evening full of romantic comedies, all designed to teach her what she needed to know about love and entrapment.

The sun began to show through the clouds by the time she had arrived back at her house, which made her smile as she unloaded her packages. She was relieved her father had his bowling league tonight, as this would allow her some time to work on reinventing herself. After a bowl of chicken noodle soup and three movies where "love triumphed," she fell asleep and dreamt of Bradley as her leading man.

LOOSE LIPS

"HEY THERE, BISCUIT. Time to rise and shine!" Maggie's father flipped on her bedroom light, causing her to squint before pulling the blanket up over her head. "Mags, we need to talk," he said, his voice full of concern. "Are you awake enough to understand me, yet?"

A deep groan came from underneath the covers.

"Good," he said. "I was watching a documentary last night on intestinal parasites. Do you realize a large number of the world's population has some type of worms? Ringworms, hookworms, pinworms. The photos they showed were disgusting! I could hardly sleep last night just thinking about those critters living inside our bodies." He cringed then continued, "The doctors on the show said if you have worms, your symptoms are fatigue, stomach pain, and gas. Well, I have noticed lately that you and I have been more tired than usual, and we both know how much gas I have. I think it might be wise for us to make an appointment with Dr. Dumont today." He swallowed hard at the thought.

These types of conversations were the norm between Maggie and her father ever since her mother had passed away. Visits to Dr. Dumont were as common as going to the grocery store, having been checked for malaria, liver disease, strokes, and rabies. Her father always said, "It is better to be safe than sorry."

Ordinarily, Maggie would be freaked out at the thought of worms crawling around in her belly, but on this day, she was spending her mental energies on tracking down "perps." She pulled the covers from her face, brushed the hair from her eyes, and sat up on one elbow. "That sounds horrible, Daddy. I saw how the old cocker spaniel that lives across the street acted when he had worms, and I sure as heck don't want to get caught draggin' my behind across the carpet to get relief. I will gladly get a checkup, but I am pretty busy this week. Any way we could go see the doc next week?"

Her father sighed heavily in frustration, but his emphasis on the importance of this matter was lost in his soft words. "Well, we shouldn't put this off any longer than that. The report said if neglected, the worms can travel to your brain and cause considerable damage." He hesitated as the thought ran scenarios through his mind, then he held up two fingers in a peace sign, four inches from her face. "Maggie, how many fingers am I holding up? Have you noticed being more forgetful than usual?"

"Daddy, I am always forgetful, so if that is one of the symptoms, it may be too late for me."

"Not funny, little missy. Intestinal parasites are not a laughing matter. I have a responsibility as your father to protect you from external and internal forces."

Maggie conceded, "I know, Daddy, and you do a great job. Let's go Monday, and maybe we can go get ice cream after that." She knew her father could never resist a sugary food source.

"That sounds terrific. I'll make the appointment." He walked over and kissed Maggie on top of her head. "I'm heading off to work now. Have a good day, sweetie. Go make the world as happy as you make me." He pulled her door shut, and moments later, she heard his car pulling out of the driveway.

Maggie stretched and let out a huge, very vocal yawn. Climbing from her bed, she turned on the television, hoping to find some crime-fighting tips while she got ready for work. As she scanned the channels, she landed on the Cartoon Network, and like a moth to a light, she became mesmerized. Lowering herself onto the couch, her eyes locked on to the animated characters on the screen as they pummeled each other. A commercial break broke the comedy's spell over her, and she realized that this indulgence was going to make her late for work if she didn't stop immediately. She pointed the remote at the television and regrettably turned it off.

Mr. Gene was completely intolerant of lateness, so Maggie not only had to speed to get to The Spot, she had to run to make it into the café door on time. She sprinted through the diner, grabbed her time card, and pulled down the lever of the time clock as it struck 10:00 a.m.

"Yeah, baby! I made it. That's right," she said, with great pride. She spun around and ran right smack into Mr. Gene's massive chest, causing her to yelp, "What in the world?"

"Cutting it awfully close there, aren't ya'?" he said, one eyebrow rising.

"I, uh, there was a Girl Scout that came to my door this morning selling cookies, and I couldn't say no to her sweet, little, innocent face."

"It's a school day. Shouldn't Girl Scouts be in class?"

Maggie knew she was quite possibly the world's worst liar, but she had already committed to her story, so she continued, "That is precisely why I couldn't say no. She was blind, so she goes to a special school, and today is National Guide Dog Day, so the dogs got the day off. Everyone knows that kids can't attend school without their dogs. Duh!"

Mr. Gene couldn't even argue with this story. It was so obviously a lie, but such an impressive one, he let her go.

The ring of the bell over the front door announced a new customer had arrived. Maggie stopped wiping the counter and turned to take a glance. It was Bradley. He headed to the booth in the corner, and she headed back into the kitchen.

"Okay," she spoke softly to herself. "What would a good cop do?" She wanted to grab herself by the collar and shake herself, hoping that would stir up any confidence she had in her body. "What if I can't keep it together? What if I slip up and tell him I saw Sylvia rustling through his boxer shorts yesterday?"

"Excuse me, are you talking to me?" Unbeknownst to Maggie, the bread delivery man had entered through the back door and was stocking the shelves with extra hamburger buns.

"How dare you eavesdrop on a poor innocent girl!" She stormed out to the dining area, completely embarrassed, leaving the very confused gentleman to continue his job.

Looking toward Bradley, a sweet smile crossed her lips. Her steps were light and slow as she started to move in his direction; her fingers tensing up at the thought of running them through his golden-brown hair. With her eyes slightly closed and her head tipped toward the side in pure bliss, she fantasized about getting close enough to smell his cologne.

Squeezing her eyes closed even tighter, her imagination completely hijacked her rational mind. The magnitude of this very bad idea was felt the second she met up with the large pillar in the middle of the diner that stood between her and Bradley. *Smack!* A deep groan escaped from her body the second her face crashed into the hard surface. A momentary pause to rub the bump that was already forming on the middle of her forehead was needed. *That is what I get for lusting after a bad person. God, are you trying to knock some sense into me?* she thought.

In an attempt to shake off the emotions that had clouded her vision, she bounced up and down from one foot to the other and shook her arms as if she was a boxer entering into the ring. "Okay, here I go." The always-friendly Maggie put on the best bad attitude she could muster up to counteract her out-of-control desires. Before arriving at the table where he was sitting, she filled a glass with ice and topped it off with sweet tea, remembering that was his drink of choice. Setting the glass in front of him, she said sharply, "What do you want to eat?"

He looked at her and smiled, "Well, good morning. Wow! What happened to your forehead?" he asked, his voice sweet with compassion.

"Oh, this?" she said, wincing as she touched the newly formed "goose egg" on her forehead. "It's nothing. Just a hairstyling accident." She was proud of herself for coming up with such an impressive excuse, thinking it made her sound like a fashionista.

He lowered his eyes from her forehead, to her name tag. "So I told you my name the other day. Mind if I call you, Maggie?"

His voice completely destroyed her self-imposed defenses, as she thought, *His voice sounds like birds singing on a spring morning.*

The tension left her body and was replaced with a warm smile. "Yes, you can call me Maggie. I am sorry I didn't introduce myself before. I just never think of telling customers my name, because everyone in town pretty much knows me."

"Well, I wanted to apologize for not having a more proper introduction last time. I hope I didn't appear rude. We were working on some very important details and it is all time sensitive, so I may have been a little impatient."

"No, I never found you rude. I thought you were very nice, actually." She blushed and nervously began to fiddle with a loose string on her pocket so as to avoid any eye contact.

Bradley missed her discomfort and continued, "And if working on this secret project isn't enough, someone broke into my hotel room yesterday. The scary part was, the room was ransacked while I was in the shower. Nothing was stolen, but I am still a little shaken up by it. It is just freaky to know there was someone lurking around my room while I was unaware, rummaging through my stuff. I reported it to the front desk, and that old guy that works there, I think his name is Sam, got real nervous and started saying something about the hotel being built on a fault line, and sometimes a tremor will shake the hotel and cause damages to certain rooms, but that just didn't sound right to me. I just wish I could catch the culprit. I would beat them with a rubber hose until they told me why they felt the need to go through my stuff."

Maggie had a shiver run up her spine, and she suddenly wished Sylvia was there to help. "Wow! That is bizarre." She had to think quickly. "You should trust porter Sam about earthquake stuff. I heard at one point in his life, he was going to college to be a seismologist but dropped out because, uh…" She took a pause to create the perfect lie, then it hit her. "Um, he dropped out because he had a lover, and she was a bully, and he had to get away from her. I heard she actually would rough him up just to get him to tell her private information! He finally gave up his dream of predicting earthquakes and started working at the hotel, just because he was tired of her choking him with his own bow tie."

Desperate to change the subject, "So where is the fellow that was with you last time you were in?"

"Oh, Mike? He was only in town for a couple days to help me iron out some really big details, but his job requires him to keep a lot of people in line, so he flew back home to 'knock some heads together.' He's my partner in crime, and I am kind of lost without him."

He leaned forward and looked around to make sure no one else could hear him. "I would love to tell you what we are planning, but it is a huge secret. Just know I am involved in something really big, and once I pull this off, everyone in this town is going to be very impressed with this guy." To emphasize his point, he used his thumbs to point at himself.

He let out a short laugh then leaned back and took a drink from his iced tea. Maggie never said a word, afraid if she said anything, he might stop sharing. He continued, "I have never been left alone to complete something this large before. It is kind of scary, but my dad is a busy man, and he spends so much of his time cleaning up messes. I am kind of flattered he thinks I have what it takes to pull this off without his help. All I need to do is get Grandma to her house, Saturday at seven o'clock, then the rest should take care of itself."

The sound of Mr. Gene yelling her name brought the conversation to an abrupt halt.

"Excuse me. I had better see what the boss needs." She skipped over to Mr. Gene, who was standing at the grill.

"Are you planning on standing there grinning at that man all day, because I have patrons in my restaurant who are about to pass out from hunger. If you want to stand and smile all day, go be a supermodel, and let me hire someone who can keep my customers from fainting."

"Oh, Mr. Gene, you are so funny. No one is going to pass out." Maggie totally missed the implications he was making.

Mr. Gene grunted. "Take these burgers to table six."

She picked up the plates and delivered them with a smile, stopping to give a clean spoon to a little boy who dropped his on the floor while eating his ice cream.

She quickly returned to Bradley's table. "Mr. Gene thinks I should get back to work, so let me tell you today's specials. We have the meatloaf dinner which comes with mashed potatoes and green beans or the 'pork-a-licious' tenderloin platter with fries. I recommend the tenderloin, because Mr. Gene puts green peppers in his meatloaf, and I think they are gross. I told him that once, but he said I wasn't old enough to have an opinion."

"Then the tenderloin it is. I appreciate your honesty as an employee of this great eatery," he said.

Aware the couple at the table beside her needed water, Maggie excused herself, stuck Bradley's order on the clip above the grill for Mr. Gene to fill, and then tended to the needs of the other customers. As she went about her business, she replayed the details of her conversation with Bradley over and over in her mind.

Somewhat surprised he trusted her enough to confess that his father was obviously the "godfather" of their local mobster branch, she shuddered at the realization that the mess he went home to clean up was probably knocking off some other unsuspecting old person.

Trying to get inside the mind of Bradley, every movie she had ever seen about mobsters replayed in her mind. "I wonder if he went through some type of initiation where he had to kiss his father's ring to vow his allegiance to the family."

All of Hollywood stereotyping almost persuaded her to give Bradley a tip and let him know he wasn't going to last long in the family business if he continued telling all of the secrets but knew that conversation would give it away that she was on to him. "Geez, doesn't he know anything about the "lady in red" who gave up Dillinger? Women are experts at bringing down the bad guys because men have loose lips when it comes to trying to impress a woman."

Mr. Gene rang the bell, announcing to Maggie her order was ready to be served. She picked up the tenderloin and huge pile of steaming hot fries from the kitchen and delivered them to Bradley's table.

As she sat down his plate, he moved his glass of sweet tea, and his hand gently brushed hers. The brush was so subtle, Bradley never even noticed it. But Maggie sure did.

"I love you," she said, softly. Her eyebrows shot straight up, and she slapped her hand over her mouth as soon as the words escaped.

"Excuse me?" he asked.

She recovered quickly. "I said, be sure and chew. I don't want you to choke on your lunch. Take small bites and chew, chew, chew. It is a proven fact, people who take smaller bites and chew their food sufficiently, live longer, probably because they won't choke to death, which would technically shorten your life."

"Oh, Maggie. You sure make me smile."

"Kind of like a circus clown?" She immediately regretted her choice of words, but when Bradley laughed out loud, she relaxed.

Leaving him with his lunch, she returned to her work, but took every opportunity to sneak a peek at him when he wasn't looking.

I could never understand why women fall for the bad boys, but I sure do now, she thought.

She watched as he wiped his mouth with his napkin and dropped it on the table. Reaching into the wallet he took from his back pocket, he pulled the necessary amount of cash needed to pay his bill. Laying the cash on the table, he turned around and caught her attention. He smiled and gave her a wave. That smile made her melt.

THE BRIEFING

Maggie was excited to get home from work, her pockets bulging from the tips she had earned that day. She was grateful the customers of the diner were so generous with her, knowing every dime made a difference to her and her father.

Upon the opening of the front door, she was met with the same familiar view of her father sleeping peacefully in his brown fake leather recliner, the unread newspaper lying across his lap. Seeing him sleep always made her smile, his fuzzy, plump cheeks making him look like a cuddly groundhog.

Picking up the newspaper from his lap, she folded it and placed it on the coffee table, taking a moment to watch his chest rise and fall with each sleepy breath.

She prayed every night, thanking God for such a great father. She also included Sylvia and Mr. Gene in those prayers, knowing they were sent from heaven to fill in for the void left by the loss of her mother. And it worked. She never felt any lack when it came to being loved and adored, and thanks to them, her life was full of joy and security.

Her thoughts went to Bradley. *I bet he never had the love that I had, and that is why he crossed over to the dark side. Since his parents are the leaders of a crime family, I'm sure they were too busy to hold him or read him a book or tell him that they were proud of him. He is doing all of these bad things because he just wants their love and acceptance. Poor fella.*

She felt terrible sadness as she considered the possibility that Bradley never felt the unconditional love she had. "I bet the love of a good woman would rehabilitate him." She giggled. "Now I am starting to sound like Sylvia."

She took the remote from the arm of the chair and turned the television off, the silence immediately waking her father from his slumber.

"Hello, my little Magpie. How was work today?" He stretched and let out a big yawn.

"It was terrific. I actually had one lady tip me five dollars, and all she had ordered was a glass of tea."

"See, Mags, you get those kinds of tips because people love you. You're the best waitress this town has ever seen. As a matter of fact, you should consider teaching classes at the junior college on how to waitress. You could—" He stopped in mid-sentence, sprang from his chair, ran over to Maggie, and grabbed her face in his hands.

"Maggie! What happened to your forehead? Were you in an accident? Oh my God, was the diner robbed? Did you get assaulted? Did a gang member try and initiate you into their group?"

"Daddy, calm down. I am fine," she said, taking his hands from her face and holding them reassuringly in hers. "I just made a quick right turn at the diner and ran smack dab into the pillar that stands in the middle of the place. I saw a few sparkles, but I am no worse for the wear. Well, except for this big knot in the middle of my forehead. I kind of look like a unicorn, huh?" She laughed, hoping her lack of concern would convince her father she was just fine.

He got very close to her and stared into her eyes. "Head injuries can be fatal, baby girl." He held his finger in the middle of her face, drawing a slow horizontal line from one side of her vision to the other. He apparently didn't like what he saw after his amateur eye exam. "Do you know who I am? I am your daddy. You are home, sweetheart, and I will take care of you now." He began stroking her hair to comfort her.

"Daddy, I know who you are, and I know where I am. I drove here, remember?" She looked deep into his eyes and said, "You have the sweetest blue eyes I've ever seen. You could stand to lose a few pounds, and a breath mint wouldn't hurt either, but you are still adorable."

He stepped back and tried to suck in his belly, but it didn't make much difference. "Do you really think I need to lose weight? Maybe I should talk to Dr. Dumont about having my cholesterol checked when we go in next week for our parasite test. Cholesterol is a killer, you know."

"Yep, it sure is. Even though you just had it checked last month, I am sure Doc Dumont would be glad to check it again if you would like. Now, if we are done with my medical exam, I need to get cookin'. What would you like for supper tonight?"

He thought for a moment and said, "Well, since I am going to the doctor next week, I might as well go ahead and eat whatever I want tonight because I'm sure he is going to put me on a diet when I go in. He always does." He looked sad about the future calorie restrictions but quickly snapped out of it when he thought, "I guess that makes tonight a free night then, so how about some fried chicken, mashed potatoes, and pan-fried gravy?"

Maggie grabbed him and kissed him on the cheek. "I love you, Daddy. Now let me take my minor head injury and get to work."

He put his arms around her and gave her a big hug that was warm, genuine, and very comfortable. "I love you too, Magpie."

The phone began ringing, pulling Maggie from her father's embrace. "I will get that in the kitchen so I can get dinner started. You sit back down and finish your newspaper. I'll yell for you when it's time to eat."

"Okay, doll face." He headed back to his chair, sat down, and began snoring almost immediately.

Maggie stepped into the kitchen and picked up the receiver of the harvest gold, rotary phone that had hung on their wall since before she was born. "Hello?" she said.

"I swear there is nothing good on this television. I don't know why I even keep it. I should unplug it and give it to the Salvation Army."

It was Sylvia, thinking out loud, not really wanting dialogue. Her rant about the lack of interesting television programming quickly turned to the real reason for the call. "So did you see 'Mr. Danger' today?"

Maggie knew exactly who she was talking about. "Yes. He came in for an early lunch and boy, oh boy, did I get the scoop!"

While she peeled potatoes and threw them into a pot of boiling water, she gave a play-by-play account of her conversation with Bradley, emphasizing and embellishing any detail she felt was necessary.

"I can't believe that boy has such loose lips," Sylvia said. "He must be new at this mob thing, and with his inability to keep a secret, it won't be long before they put a horse's head in his bed!"

"Sylvia! Don't you say that! He seems like a perfectly nice man who is most likely being forced into something he does not want to do. He is in over his head, and it is obvious he is only doing this because he wants to please his horrible father. I think we need to consider that the evil one here is not Bradley."

"Girl, how in the world would you make it through this life without me?" Sylvia let out a heavy sigh in disbelief. "You have been watching too much Dr. Phil. Bradley doesn't have daddy issues, and you can't rehabilitate this criminal. He is just a rotten apple."

"Oh, Sylvia, this is terrible. I'm just having such a hard time believing all of this. He seems so nice."

"I'm glad you feel that way. I want you to harness all of those warm and fuzzy feelings, and turn them into sexual energy. Don't get me wrong. I don't want you getting all goo-goo eyed for 'Mr. Tough Stuff', but I do need you to use the obvious chemistry that is between you two to find out more info. Shoot, at this point, I think you could talk this man into buying ice, even if he was an Eskimo. You just need to stay focused. Remember, once we save this woman's life, it will be all over the television, and you will get your pick of any man."

"I guess I have a responsibility as an American to stop this immoral person," Maggie said, bravely.

"Exactly! Now it is time for us to turn up the heat. I need you to get Bradley to fall in love with you."

"No. Absolutely not! I am not capable of that."

"Stop saying you can't and tell me you can." Sylvia, speaking like a drill sergeant, waited for a reply but heard nothing but silence on the other end of the phone line.

Sylvia began again. "Maggie? I said tell me you can."

"I hope I can," Maggie replied, weakly.

"I said tell me you can!" Sylvia said, even more forcefully this time.

"I can."

"Louder!"

"I can."

"This time with feeling!"

"I can!" Maggie surprised herself at how truly convincing she sounded.

"Great. Now, I have to go to the chiropractor tomorrow, so you call me in the afternoon and let me know how you set the trap."

"Okay. I'll call you."

As Maggie hung up the receiver, the potatoes began to boil over, making a loud hiss as the water hit the flames coming from the stoves burner.

"Well, fiddlesticks!" she replied, turning the fire off underneath the pan to stop the eruption.

THAT NEW BRA REALLY WORKED

Ring! Ring! Maggie rolled over and whacked the alarm clock to silence it but the annoying sound continued. *Ring! Ring!* She picked up the clock and shook it to try and alleviate the problem but no luck. Perplexed, she was forced to sit up. *What in the world is wrong with my clock?* she thought.

Ring! Ring! Holding on to the clock made it perfectly clear to her sleepy mind that the sound was not coming from the bedside time piece but from the telephone on the dresser. She dropped the clock on the bed and dove for the phone. "Hello?"

Sylvia's voice was on the other end. "Get up, you lazy bag of bones. The day is half over already."

"Sylvia, it is only six thirty in the morning."

"That is what I said. Half over. I have already done two loads of laundry, waxed my upper lip and chin, and did my aerobic exercises. I was going to hang my sheets out to dry, but Mr. Newsome volunteered to do it for me. Something about it being a 'privilege to touch the bedding upon which I lay.' Whatever! So what time do you work today?"

"I'm supposed to go in at noon."

"What if you miss Bradley? We are on a deadline here. We don't have a lot of time left, and we have very little information to go on."

"I know, and that is why I volunteered to go to work early. Mr. Gene has been barking about the mess in the storage cabinet for the last year, so I volunteered to come in early and organize it."

"Great idea! Now you are thinking like a detective."

"Yep, I sure am. And you will also be glad to know, I am ready to take on the assignment you gave me yesterday. I made a purchase that'll guarantee I will have Bradley eating out of my hand by the end of the day. When he sees me wearing my new "sex kitten" push-up bra, he won't stand a chance."

"What the…? Sex kitten! Oh dear! Maggie, you are in over your head. You are going to hurt yourself or someone else. I am going to get ready and take the bus into town. I'll meet you at the diner."

"No. I am fine. Actually, I am more than fine. I am terrifically fine. I will call you later and let you know what I find out."

"Be careful. He is dangerous, and I don't want to see on the nightly news that they found your body dumped in the river."

Maggie swallowed hard. Her graphic comment was just another reminder the stakes were really high in this game.

"I will be careful, and don't worry. Mr. Gene would never let anything happen to me. He loves me."

"You would have to have a heart to love someone, and that man is hollow on the inside."

"I have told you before. Mr. Gene loves in his own way."

"Yeah, he loves like a nasty, old, rabid pit bull!"

"Hey, pit bulls can be loving. Don't stereotype."

"I can honestly say, Maggie, I have never met anyone like you."

"I know. You tell me that all the time. Now I have a job to do. I must go put Bradley under my spell. I'll call you later."

"Don't you dare forget!"

"How could I ever forget you, Sylvia?"

"True. I am pretty unforgettable, huh?"

Maggie hung up the phone and headed upstairs to her room to begin her transformation. A shower was the first priority, followed by a slathering of her body with rose-scented lotion that was normally used when she attended weddings and funerals. After slipping into her new bra, she gave her most sexy pose in front of the mirror. "Hmm, these bras do lift and separate!" Somewhat saddened she had to cover her new bra with her plain uniform, she boldly left the top button open, something she never had to courage to do before.

Sitting down at her vanity, she pulled out the fancy boxes of makeup she had purchased the day before. After a blur of brushes, blotting, and tissues, she settled on her third reapplication. Despite the distinctive makeup line across her neck, the lipstick on her teeth, and the mascara that had somehow gotten on her forehead, she felt awesome as she walked into The Spot.

"Morning, Mr. Gene. How are you doing on this lovely day?"

Mr. Gene looked up from the eggs he was scrambling.

"I am—" His mouth dropped open, his eyebrows shot up, and he stopped in mid-sentence. "Little Maggie" stood before him, no longer as a little girl but as a young lady.

Recognizing his surprised expression, she was flooded with feelings of self-consciousness. "Is there something wrong?" She tugged on her uniform top that was strangely gaping between the buttons, thanks to her new push-up bra.

"Wrong? Not wrong. Just different."

"What do you mean, different?" Her insecurities were growing.

"Oh, I don't mean you. I just heard an odd sound, and I was surprised when I turned around and saw you." He was trying hard to cover the awkwardness, but doing such a lousy job, he finally fessed up.

"Did your father see you before you left home today?"

"No, sir. Why? Do I look funny?" She continued tugging on her uniform and began looking for a napkin to wipe off some of her makeup.

"No. You do not look funny at all, but maybe you should put on a sweater. It is chilly today, and I don't want you to get sick because I just know you will end up sneezing all over my customers, and I will end up going broke because you started your own epidemic."

Mr. Gene took an old jacket from the coat rack in the back of the restaurant. It had not been worn in several years and smelled like old grease. He shook the dust off of it and dropped it over her shoulders.

"Here, put this on. And button it up tightly."

Owning her new look, she replied, "Mr. Gene, it is a beautiful spring day. All of the snow is gone, the trees are blooming, and the sun is shining brightly. I will be sweating like a pig if I wear this jacket all day. But thank you for caring."

She removed the garment and flung it over her arm. Reaching up, she gave Mr. Gene a hug around the neck.

Grumbling something about "girls these days," he dropped his head and walked back to the grill.

Maggie hung the jacket back on the coat rack and went to the supply cabinet to begin the task of organizing the mountain of spices, oils, and containers of unknown ingredients that had been sitting there as long as she could remember. Some of the packages looked older than her.

Remaining focused on the reason she came in to work early was no easy task, stopping every time the bell above the front door rang to see who was coming in or going out. After a good hours worth of wiping the dust off of shelves and bottles, the bell rang again, and this time it was Bradley. Maggie watched as he took a seat in the booth near the door.

"There's no turning back now," she said under her breath.

Rubbing her lips together like she had seen Sylvia do on many occasions, she slipped her hand into her top to pull her bra straps back up onto her shoulders.

Boy, this bra really does make a girl feel like a million bucks, she thought, walking into the dining area with a swagger she never had before.

Alma—a somewhat antisocial, unattractive lady that worked as a waitress three days a week for Mr. Gene—had already given Bradley his menu and a glass of water and had left to submit his order when Maggie arrived. "Well, hello there, big boy," she said in a breathy voice. Looking over the water glass he was drinking from, he caught a glimpse of her "new and improved" version and gasped. *Cough! Cough!*

Cough! Whatever water wasn't running down his chin had been spewed directly onto her.

"Oh, I am so sorry," he said to the now dripping-wet Maggie, "I don't know what happened." He grabbed his napkin and nervously began blotting the water off of her arms and shoulders but froze when he got to her chest. He could not look her in the eyes, and this time, he was the one blushing. Taking the napkin from his hand, she blotted the wettest areas, drying herself off the best she could. He sat back down and began fiddling with his silverware.

"Thank you for the lovely shower," Maggie said, wanting to break the tension.

"I guess I must have choked on something. Went down the wrong pipe maybe."

"Don't worry about it. I have sprayed many people in my lifetime. I will dry."

She plopped down on the seat in the booth, across from him. "So what have you been doing since I saw you last?" She looked across the table at him, winked, and nodded. Desiring to appear engaging and alluring, the only thing she was really feeling was silly and awkward.

He looked up from the menu. "Got something in your eye?" he asked, oblivious to her flirting.

Mr. Gene, yelling her name from the kitchen, saved her from having to answer the question.

"Maggie! Come here now!"

"Yes, sir," she yelled back. She stood up and excused herself, adding a little extra wiggle in her walk in the hopes Bradley was watching. She strolled to where Mr. Gene stood, with his ever-present spatula in his hand.

"Who is that man you are talking to? He looks shady, if you ask me," he said suspiciously, his eyebrows scrunched together. "I am beginning to find it odd that every time I look out there, I see you yacking it up with him. What is the story?"

"Well, Sylvia asked me—" she stopped herself, not wanting to give him any information, knowing if he found out the truth, he would probably march out into the dining room, tie Bradley up with a kitchen towel, and hold him captive until the police came. This possibility caused her to change her story from truth to a humongous lie.

"Well, the truth is"—she looked to the ground as she wove this tale, knowing if she looked Mr. Gene in the eyes, he would see right through her—"he is in town, selling, um, chainsaws. Yeah, chainsaws, and the profit he earns is going to pay for his great-aunt's hip surgery."

Convinced he was falling for it, she continued, "You know me. I just can't pass up helping out a neighbor in distress, and coincidentally, my father always needed a good chainsaw, so I am talking to this nice gentleman about his payment plan."

Mr. Gene didn't even crack a smile. "Chainsaws? Really? That weasel out there is selling chainsaws?" Calling her bluff, he said, "Well, I could use a good chainsaw myself. Maybe I will go visit with him and see what kind of deal he will offer me."

She responded, "Oh, what a bummer! I wish I would have known you needed one, because I just bought his last one. I could ask him if he has any complementary screw-driver sets left."

Mr. Gene was a man with very little patience on a good day, so to expect him to continue listening to her story was unrealistic.

"Listen here, Missy! I know that Sylvia has put you up to something, and it has nothing to do with a chainsaw. So you get back out there and know I am watching you. And if that man makes one squirrely move, I will be on him faster than stink on a turd. Now, your shift has officially begun, so quit wasting time out there with that rat and take this BLT to the man at table six."

Maggie knew he meant business and did not stay around to defend her story. "Yes, sir."

She took the plate with the sandwich and walked back out onto the floor, but not before adjusting her bra straps that had slid back down from her shoulders. Refilling glasses, taking orders, and visiting with customers kept her busy while Bradley finished his meal, she felt a little bit of panic knowing Sylvia was not going to be happy she had completely failed in her mission. Even more disappointing was that this failure came despite the new bra and makeup.

Bradley picked up his ticket, looked at the price, then reached for his wallet.

She adjusted her bra straps up again and grabbed the toothpick dispenser from beside the cash register. "Here you go, Bradley. Have a toothpick." she said, as she shoved the shiny box of tooth cleaners towards his face. "Studies have shown, good dental hygiene can add up to five years to your life."

He politely took one of the toothpicks. "I am glad you came over because there was something I wanted to ask you. Since I am only going to be around for another week or so, I would love to know more about this little town before I have to leave. I was wondering if maybe you had some time you could show me some of the hot spots in town."

"Sure. There is the Playmore Bowling Alley on Third Street. Then there is the Plaza Theater on Mitchell."

"No, Maggie. I'm not asking you to tell me where these things are. I would like for you to show me. And truthfully,

I would also like to get to know a little more about you, as well. Are you busy tonight?"

Wow! This bra really does work, she thought. She tried to act calm, but her thoughts were freaking out. *What do I do? If I say yes and he has figured out that I am onto him, he may want to pick me up in his car so he can knock me on the head and dump my body in the river, like Sylvia said. I have always wanted to see the river, but I would prefer to be conscious when I get there.*

She reeled her thoughts back in and made herself focus on making a safe plan. "How about we meet at the movie theatre? It is the most happening place here in town. I will drive myself and meet you there because I just never know if I am going to get out of here on time. Mr. Gene is really good at finding new projects for me to do, right at closing time."

"Sounds great. What time should we meet?"

"Let's say, seven thirty."

The mystery surrounding this date made her feel exotic and sexy, so she added, "I will be wearing a pink scarf, so you will be able to recognize me in the crowd." She batted her eyes and took her hand and flicked her hair from her shoulder seductively.

Bradley let out a giggle but realized quickly she wasn't laughing along with him.

He looked at her and said, "Don't worry, Maggie. To me, you always stand out in a crowd." It was hard to tell who was more shocked by his admission. Him, or her. They stood silently, neither one knowing what to say next to move past the awkward embarrassment they were both feeling. Bradley finally spoke, "I…um…you…um…See ya later tonight!"

Maggie never moved, standing in the middle of the floor with a silly grin on her face.

"Maggie! The food won't serve itself. Get to work or you're fired!"

As if deflating from the top down, her head dropped, her shoulders slumped, and an audible sigh left her body. The moment was over, thanks to Mr. Gene. "You got it, boss," she said, flashing him a forgiving grin before stacking the dirty plates on table 3.

IT'S NOT A DATE, IT'S A FACT-FINDING MISSION

Distraction is not a good thing, especially when you're a waitress, Maggie thought at the end of her shift after she had delivered the wrong order to two tables, caught the string of her apron on fire while standing too close to the grill, and accidentally filling all the ketchup bottles with steak sauce. Her mind had not really been on her work, instead, all of her mental energies were spent thinking about the first real date she was about to attend.

Adrenaline and excitement causing her to drive even faster than normal, she arrived safely at home. Knowing she had only a short time to change clothes and spruce up before meeting Bradley, she wasted no time getting into the house. Upon entering, she first checked for her father and found him snoring in his recliner. Relieved she had time to make a private call, she dialed Sylvia's number. The ringing stopped after only one ring. "Hello."

"Wow, that was quick."

"Quick? That is your perspective! I have been sitting here all afternoon waiting for you, so I would not say anything about this call was quick."

"I am sorry, but you know how busy 'hot beef Thursday' can be. And then Mr. Gene had me—"

Sylvia interrupted, "Don't waste time. Give me the details about what information you got out of that slimy dog Bradley?"

Maggie was apprehensive to tell Sylvia the truth, but she knew there was no way she could keep a secret this big from her best friend. "I did not get as much info as I would have liked to, but I am going to try harder…tonight."

"Tonight?" Sylvia shouted.

"Yes, he asked me out on a date."

"Oh, my goodness. Abort the mission. Abort! You have now crossed into uncharted territory, and you are incapable of handling a task this big. Don't you dare leave that house. I once knew a guy…"

Maggie recognized that conversation starter as the beginning of a lengthy life story, and she had no intention of canceling, so she softly laid the receiver on the bed and went about changing out of her work clothes. Thinking the new bra was a definite asset, she decided to keep it on. After pulling a fuzzy, pink sweater over her head, she stepped into her tightest jeans and jumped up and down several times before she was able to get them buttoned around her waist. Finishing her outfit with a pink and purple checked scarf that she loosely draped around her neck, she smiled as she saw her reflection in the mirror.

She picked up the phone, and Sylvia was still talking. "…and he never did return!" Maggie had no idea what the beginning of that story was but did not have time to ask. "Sylvia, I am a big girl now, and even more importantly, I am a crime fighter. You have taught me so much, and I know I am more than able to take care of myself. It will be in a public location, so what could go wrong?"

"What could go wrong?" Sylvia repeated. "Let's start with you disappearing. As skinny as you are, he could throw you over his shoulder and carry you away before anyone even noticed. I keep telling you to eat more because fat people are harder to kidnap. I would love to see some punk try and get me into a car. All I need to do is think "dead weight", and there would be no way someone could wrestle me into a—"

Maggie, aware of the time, interrupted. "I promise I will be careful, but now, I have to go. Don't want to be late for my first date, I mean, my first fact-finding mission. I will call you as soon as I get home." She hung up before Sylvia could say anything else.

One last thing needed to be done before leaving. She opened the drawer of her dresser and pulled out the bottle of perfume Sylvia had given her for her birthday. The note was still attached to it, written in her friend's distinct handwriting. It read, "This perfume has magical powers on men, so use it sparingly. A dab behind each ear and a touch near your cleavage, and you can make a man do tricks like a trained monkey."

Deciding if three dabs were good, five splashes would be better, she drenched herself in the amber-colored liquid, put on another coat of lipstick, and looked in the mirror. "I sure wish my first date was not with someone who was about to be a member of the penal system."

Before leaving, she gently shook her father's arm to wake him. "Daddy? I am going with Sylvia to the movies, so don't wait up."

He yawned before replying, "Okay, baby girl. Take your sanitary wipes. Movie theater seats are some of the dirtiest surfaces in the world."

"Good idea. I have them in my purse, and I will make sure I wipe them off before we sit down. No one wants a nasty case of staph infection." She kissed him on the forehead and headed out the door, pulling it shut behind her. Taking a moment to catch her breath on the front porch, she thought, *I am going on a date with a mobster, I just lied to my father, and I'm wearing a "sex-kitten" push-up bra. I don't even know myself anymore.* Smiling, she headed to her car.

Bradley was standing valiantly by the front door of the theatre when she arrived. "You look very nice tonight," he said as she walked up to greet him.

Maggie curtsied and tipped her head coyly to the side. "Well, thank you, kind sir," she said with a southern drawl. "I got this shirt on sale for three dollars."

Bradley snickered, "I think it was well worth the money. You look terrific. Should we go inside?"

"Lead the way," she said, hoping her nervously wobbly legs would carry her to the location he chose.

IT PLAYED LIKE A BAD MOVIE

"Jake, that girl has gone and gotten herself in trouble." The contented canine exhaled deeply, his eyes not even opening in response to Sylvia's comment. "Why in the world wouldn't she listen to me? I have told her over and over, I know it all because I have done it all. She is making such unwise decisions! I have no choice but to go to the theater and provide backup for her, so she doesn't go and get herself kidnapped. Good thing for her, I really wanted to see the movie that's playing anyway. I just need to pull together a few items first. I don't want her to think I am checking up on her, so I am going to need a good disguise." Leaving Jake where he lay, she stepped into her bedroom to find the perfect accessories to make her unrecognizable to the person in the world that knew her best.

The commotion coming from her room caused Jake to lift his head in concern. Within a short time, the noises stopped, and Sylvia emerged wearing a pair of dark sunglasses and a waist-long blond wig she had gotten as part of a Lady Godiva costume. "See ya later, Jake," she said, stepping over her canine, "Gotta get goin' if I'm gonna catch the bus."

The bus doors opened in front of the theatre, and she stepped off. Quickly surveying the location to make sure she was not going to be seen by her friend, she adjusted her wig and glasses, then stepped up to the ticket window. "I'll take one, please."

The teenage girl behind the glass spoke with a very pronounced lisp due to her newly-acquired tongue piercing. Sylvia watched, mesmerized, as the young lady tried to talk and still twirl the glistening gold ball on the rod that was stuck through her tongue. "One at a 'thenior prithe'?" she asked.

"Thenior? I mean, senior? Why would you assume I was a senior?" Sylvia bristled at the accusation of being old.

The girl leaned forward to get a better look at Sylvia's lower half then leaned back in her seat. "Becauth you look juth like my grandma. Mine-uth the bad wig."

"Can your grandma kick your butt? Because I sure can! I work out every day, little missy!" Punctuating her statement with proof, she pulled up the sleeve of her house dress to show her flexed bicep.

"Calm down before you buthed an artery," the teen said, unafraid of Sylvia's threats. "I will juth charge you regular prithe, which, by the way, is double the thenior prithe. Now, are you happy?"

Mumbling under her breath, Sylvia pulled out her crocheted coin purse from her bag. "I think the hole they drilled in your tongue let any sense of reason you had pour out. It doesn't take a rocket scientist to tell you that I am by no means a senior." Yanking the ticket from the hand of the speech-impeded teen after paying full price, Sylvia defiantly leaned closer to the glass that separated the two. Not to be intimidated, the young girl leaned close and began clacking the gold ball piercing against her teeth. Sylvia stepped back and said, "Well played."

Walking through the doors of the theater, the smell of popcorn was like a magnet, pulling her directly to the snack counter. "Goody! The lines are short. I better get me a couple snacks to keep my strength up in case I have to rumble with that good-for-nothing Bradley." Stepping in line behind a middle-aged couple, she took off her sunglasses to get a better look at the menu.

"Oh, honey," the lady spoke sweetly to her husband, "I would love some popcorn, but what size should we get? You know, if we get the small one, we will have to come back to get a refill before the show is over. But if we get a large one, we will get full and not be able to go out for dinner later."

He pinched her cheek, "Pookie, you are so right. I will get my princess a medium-sized popcorn. How is that, my darling?"

"Honey bear, you are so wonderful to me." She reached up and gave him a peck on the cheek.

Sylvia, not impressed with the mushy display, interrupted the love fest. "Excuse me, I'm sorry to be a bother, but if you wouldn't mind, could I go ahead of you? I can make my purchase and be out of your way in a flash." She squeezed in between the man and woman, moving towards the counter, not waiting for their approval. The lovebirds stood there, mouths wide open, as Sylvia brazenly began her order.

"Yes, I would like the 'super gut-buster combo' with extra butter and a Dr. Pepper. Also, throw in a box of Milk Duds, please."

The oily, teenaged boy working behind the counter had one earpiece of his iPod headphones stuck in his left ear, the other piece strategically tucked in his collar, his head bobbing to the beat of a song only he could hear. He reached down under the counter and placed a large roll of Sweet Tarts in front of Sylvia. She slid them back across the counter. "No, son, I said Milk Duds."

Never missing a beat to the song he was jamming to, he took the Sweet Tarts from the counter, reached down, and replaced them with a box of gummy bears.

Not wanting to draw attention since she was on a stakeout, she calmed herself. "Fine, I'll take those. Could I get my large combo, please?"

He took the metal scoop from inside the popcorn machine, and filled a small sack with the fluffy, white snack, and handed it to Sylvia. "Would you like a Diet Coke with that?"

She reached up and yanked the earpiece from his ear, and snapped, "Do I look like a woman that drinks Diet Coke? And a small popcorn? For goodness sakes! I said the super gut-buster!"

"Well, you might consider the smaller size, because from where I am standing, it looks like you could stand to lose a few pounds."

She grabbed the tiny bag of popcorn he had placed in front of her and, in a flash, threw it at the prepubescent punk. No longer concerned about anonymity, she said, "I demand to see your manager!"

"Sure," he said, before yelling across the lobby, "Dad, this crotchety, old lady wants to talk with you."

A thin, very pale man came out from behind a door labeled "office." As he approached the situation, the young man with the terrible customer service skills stepped out from behind the counter and stood across from Sylvia, his arms folded across his chest, smiling smugly at her.

"What seems to be the problem, ma'am?" the father asked.

"Well, you're spawn here has no manners. And don't even get me started on how bad he sucks at his job."

"I am sorry you feel that way, but I can assure you he has been thoroughly trained by the best. He is my son after all." He looked at his male-child and smiled proudly.

"Sir, I have no doubt you are a fine business owner, but I tell you, your son has the IQ of a turnip."

"Daddy, I was doing a beautiful job, just like you taught me, and she assaulted me for no good reason," the teen spoke in a childlike voice, building his defense against Sylvia.

She fired back, "No good reason? You called me fat!"

"I didn't call you fat. I just implied that you could stand to push away from the table a bit."

Sylvia looked at his father with fire in her eyes. He grinned and let out a nervous laugh, "He gets his sassiness from his mother's side. I know very well not to comment on a woman's weight or, in your case, perfect body shape."

The compliment went unnoticed by Sylvia, who went on to give council. "In my day, we would take a boy who is as mouthy as your rotten child, turn them over our knee, and give them an attitude adjustment."

"Yeah, old lady, but in your day, dinosaurs roamed the earth and fire hadn't been invented yet." The teen laughed at his own wittiness.

The father gasped. Sylvia looked at him and said, "Well, if you're not going to do anything about this disrespect, I will." She reached up, grabbed the boy by the ear, and pulled him across the lobby. He began crying, "Help! Daddy, save me!"

Sylvia never even slowed down until she reached the bench setting against the wall at the end of the lobby. Catching the lad off guard when she plopped down, he had no choice but to follow the tug she gave him as she yanked him onto her lap. "This is what your father should have done to you a long time ago!" She took her hand and gave him a stinging swat on his behind.

"Help! Daddy! Make this mean woman stop!" he screamed.

A crowd had now formed as the teenaged clerk cried like a fourth-grade girl. Two security guards who worked at the theater quickly grabbed the boy from Sylvia's grasp. He ran to his father and buried his head into his parent's chest. "There, there, son. It's okay now," his father said, patting him on the back. "That mean old lady will not hurt you anymore."

Sylvia yelled across the theatre at the pair, "I am not old!"

One of the security guards spoke, "Excuse me, ma'am. You have been asked by the owner of this establishment to leave immediately, and we have two ways of doing this. The easy way or the hard way."

His threat did not affect her in the least because she knew she had a weapon she always successfully used against men, and it wasn't her gun. It was her flirt. Stepping up to the guard, she began batting her eyes taking her hand and running it up and down his arm. "Wow, would you look at those muscles? You are so strong. Do you work out?"

"Excuse me?" he questioned, somewhat shaken by her advances. "Ma'am, I am sorry but you have been asked by the owner of this establishment to leave. I don't want to force you to exit, but I will if you do not leave voluntarily. Please step outside."

"Are you going with me, lover boy?" She reached up and stroked his hair. "I never could resist a man in uniform." She tucked her arm under his, looking as if she was about to be escorted down the aisle of a wedding, as he nodded toward the other guard, who promptly locked his arm through Sylvia's other arm that had been dangling freely. All it took was another nod from the guard, and they lifted Sylvia straight in the air, her feet dangling above the ground.

When the realization hit her that she was about to be thrown out, she began to struggle, causing her to drop her purse, her blonde wig flying off and landing behind the guards. "Help me! Someone! Police brutality!"

"Ma'am, we are not police officers."

She looked closer and changed her cry. "Movie theater security brutality!" she shouted.

Her cries were short-lived, as the walk to outside the building was a short one. Without a single word, the guards uncoiled their arms from hers and returned to their post inside the theater, leaving her standing alone on the sidewalk.

Junior opened the door, tossed her wig and purse at her feet, and laughed maniacally. He continued laughing as he pulled the door closed behind him.

"Hey, I never got my popcorn!" She yelled, picking up her wig and placing it back on her head. Parting the long fake hair that hung over her face, she tried to smooth it into some sort of style as she walked towards the convenience store where the bus stop was located.

"Well, I can't watch the movie, but I can still get my refreshments." She walked inside the store and quickly found what she was looking for. Retrieving a large bag of popcorn and a super-sized Dr. Pepper, she made a trip down the candy aisle, picking up a large box of gummy bears. "That movie brat was right. These were a better choice." Paying for her snacks before heading back outside, she took a seat on the bench to wait for the bus to take her home.

Shoving a handful of popcorn in her mouth, she said to herself, "Kids these days need discipline. They should have more respect for their elders."

ICE CREAM SEEMS SAFE ENOUGH

THE RINGING IN Maggie's ears, a typical symptom when she was nervous, kept her from hearing any of the movie. Not that hearing would have made much of a difference; since she spent so much of the time fidgeting, she had worked up a sweat, causing her bangs to stick to her forehead, and big wet circles had formed under her arms, completely sweating through her three-dollar top. She noticed Bradley must have been having his own perspiration issues as he kept trying to dry his palms off by wiping them on his jeans.

The credits had finished rolling and the lights of the theater came back on, as the couple sat awkwardly in their seats, staring at the blank screen. He broke the silence, nervously asking, "I passed an ice cream shop on my way here. It looked like a nice place. You know anything about it?"

Maggie wanted to jump up and down, excited that a trip to get ice cream meant the date was not over yet, but she dialed back her enthusiasm, reminding herself she was with a mobster. Not a potential suitor, but a big slimy snake. Still, she thought going for ice cream seemed safe enough, even with someone who had the moral depravity of Bradley.

The ice cream store he mentioned, she knew very well; the proprietors being longtime friends of her family. Decorated in pink and white, the building was owned by Jim and Janice Wickham. They were an elderly couple, a fact that made her slightly nervous, knowing Bradley obviously liked his victims to be older.

Not wanting to share any details that might imply they had weaknesses, thus setting them up to be robbed by a thug who would use their hard-earned money to buy weapons on the black market, she chose her words carefully. "Yes, I know that store. It is called the DairySweet, and it is one of the most secure places in all of the Midwest. They have high-tech surveillance cameras, a ferocious German shepherd who is trained to respond only to German commands, and, coincidentally, Officer Larry lives on the same block so he drives by the place all the time." She looked at him, hoping for some type of reassurance that she had convinced him they were off limits.

He looked at her, a very puzzled expression on his face. "That's good, I guess. Their patrons should be safe in a place like that." He hesitated before asking, "So would you like to accompany me to get a cone?"

Maggie justified her answer with the knowing that nothing bad could really happen at such a happy place, so she gladly accepted. "Sure, but I can't stay long. I have the early shift at the diner tomorrow."

A huge smile came across Bradley's face. "Really? I mean, awesome! Do you want to ride with me? I will bring you back to your car as soon as we are finished."

Maggie knew if she was really going to get any information, she was going to have to take a gamble and spend some time with this criminal. Alone. Besides that, he smelled so good it was becoming intoxicating. "I need to go to my car first and get something, if that is okay."

"No problem," he said. "I will go with you."

Their pace seemed hurried, and upon arrival at her vehicle, she said, "You stay here on the sidewalk. Sometimes a girl needs a moment of privacy."

Bradley obliged, staying put as she climbed into her car. She reached into her purse and pulled out a crumpled receipt from the bottom of it. Shaking the purse till her hand reached the bottom, she felt around until she recognized the feel of the ink pen she had accidentally taken from the drive-through at the bank, a couple weeks before. "I really need to return this pen," she said quietly as a reminder to herself.

She clicked the pen and began to write on the scrap piece of paper.

> I, Maggie, do solemnly swear, at 9:27 PM, on this March 30th, I am getting into a black Buick, owned by Bradley Jensen. If I am never seen again, he asked me to go to the ice cream store owned by Mr. and Mrs. Wickham. I am wearing a pink sweater, denim jeans, and black and white tennis shoes. I am also wearing a scarf that makes me look very sophisticated. My jacket is brown corduroy with a huge mustard stain on the front because I had a corn dog for lunch yesterday, and it fell off the stick. If I do come up missing and this becomes my last will and testament, please get the description of my kidnapper from Sylvia Coy. She knows Bradley very well, and she has watched a lot of detective shows

> so she knows how to comply with the police if they want to do an artist's rendering of the perpetrator. Also, please tell my dad, Mr. Gene, and Sylvia, I love them. Signed, Maggie.

She took a deep breath, laid the note on the seat, and climbed out of the vehicle.

"Okay, let's go," she said, as much an encouragement to herself as an invite to Bradley. Walking slowly and silently to his vehicle, he stepped ahead of Maggie to open the passenger door for her. "Thank you, kind sir," she said before seating herself safely in his car. She rubbed her hands back and forth on top of her thighs, hoping to warm up her cold hands as well as to stop the shaking of her knees, anything to try and calm herself.

Bradley climbed in beside her, and buckled his seat belt before starting the car. Trying not to stare, she couldn't help but glance over at him. She thought, *Oh my golly, he is so cute, and he has such great manners. Certainly criminals don't open the door for a lady. Well, unless they are trying to push them out when they are driving down the highway, but that is for exits not entrances. Who knows, maybe if Sylvia and I can keep him from committing a felony, he will make someone a great husband someday. Maybe that someone could be me.* She quickly turned to look out the window to keep him from seeing her cheeks flush, and noticed a blond woman sitting on the bench at the bus stop. She spun around to take a second look out the back window.

"That is funny. Did you see the lady sitting at the bus stop? She looked so much like Sylvia, I would have bet money they were sisters, which is funny because she doesn't have any sisters. Guess my pupils have not fully dilated from being in that dark movie theater." She paused for a moment, the thought of any eye disorder, causing her to panic. This new adrenaline spike, added to her constant simmering anxiety when she was anywhere near Bradley, came out as nervous rambling, "I wonder if I should have my eyes checked. Do you think they should be dilated by now? It does seem like it is taking them an awfully long time to focus. Do you know if they do eye exams in the emergency room this late at night?" She covered one eye with her hand then switched to covering the other eye to check for any blurriness.

Bradley giggled. "I am sure your eyes are just fine. They seem perfectly healthy and beautiful to me."

She stared straight ahead, locking into memory what he had just said, her fear replaced by a sudden burst of joy.

The ride to the DairySweet was a short one, and upon arrival, Bradley stepped ahead to open the door of the parlor to let Maggie enter first.

Mr. Wickham, who was as round as he was tall, was restocking the sugar cones upon their arrival. Wearing his traditional white apron with a huge pink ice cream cone embroidered on the front, his ensemble would have not been complete without his folded paper hat that was always perched atop his thinning gray hair.

"Well, hello, Miss Maggie Bug. How in the world are you? How's your papa? He hasn't been in for his usual 'banana-split-made-with-chocolate-ice-cream-hold-the-nuts' for over a week."

"Both he and I are fine, sir. The doctor told Daddy that his cholesterol is a little high, so he has given up ice cream for a very short while."

"You go home and tell your daddy that my ice cream is like medicine. It has healing qualities, so it only does the body good. People don't need all that Prozac. They just need Rocky Road." He laughed at his own joke, his demeanor suddenly changing when he notice Bradley standing close to Maggie. "So who is this strapping young man? Is this your boyfriend?" He did not allow for an answer; instead, he squinted his eyes to get a better look. Not liking what he saw, he began his interrogation.

"Young fella, let me fill you in on something. If you are considering any kind of funny business in regards to our little Maggie, just know I may look old and feeble, but when I was in the military, I was quite a scrapper. Even though I retired with full military benefits twenty-seven years ago, I haven't lost a step. Consider yourself warned." He did some quick air boxing, fists flailing in the air. He wheezed then followed it with a coughing fit, bringing his display of virility to an abrupt end.

Maggie quickly intervened to help Mr. Wickham save his pride. "Wow, Mr. Wickham! I am so impressed. Thank you for caring so much, but there may be a misunderstanding here. Bradley is not my boyfriend. He is just visiting from out of town, and he is only here for a few days. He just wanted the best ice cream in town, and I knew this was the place to come."

Bradley stuck his hand out to politely shake the old man's hand, "Hello, sir, my name is Bradley Jensen. It is good to meet you. This is a very nice store you have here."

Mr. Wickham accepted Bradley's handshake but did not let it go after the appropriate amount of time. Instead, in an act of domination, he grasped it tightly and squeezed, his teeth clenched and his body slightly trembling from all the force he was applying.

Bradley, unaffected by the hand press, looked to Maggie for help, and she once again intervened. "My goodness, I am starving. How about you fix me up one of those triple scoop, German chocolate, ice cream sundaes with hot fudge?"

Mr. Wickham stared into Bradley's eyes, his head slowly and methodically nodding, as if he knew something his prey didn't. He slowly released his hand. "I will be keeping my eyes on you." He punctuated his warning by forming his index and middle finger into a *V*, pointing to his own eyes then pointing them toward Bradley's.

Maggie suddenly realized what she had ordered. Concerned about looking like a dainty lady, she knew she needed to change her order to something with fewer calories. "Please skip the cherry. I'm watching my figure." She took her hand and patted her almost concave stomach.

Mr. Wickham said with great conviction, "You aren't becoming anorexic, are you? I read about that crazy stuff in one of those women's magazines Janice always has lying around. I told her, I know the cure for that disease. Whipped cream!" Completely ignoring her request, he said, "Tonight, I'm gonna give you an extra-large helping of the fluffy stuff, then I am going to top it off with some glazed toasted almonds just to make sure you stay healthy. That dessert would take the anorexia out of a supermodel!"

He looked to Bradley with a snarl, "And what will you be having, Romeo?"

"I would like an extra-thick strawberry malt made with real strawberries, please."

Mr. Wickham shook his head, seemingly disgusted by the mere sight of Bradley, but swallowed his pride and began preparing the frozen confections.

Finishing off the order by sticking a straw into the glass full of thick frozen goodness, Mr. Wickham handed it to

Bradley and said to him, "It's your lucky day, stud. Not only because you are in the presence of someone as good as Maggie, but you get the 25 percent discount she always gets because she's like my own daughter. Cappeesh?" he said, cracking his knuckles before punching his right hand into his left.

Bradley, trying desperately to ignore the implications, pulled out his wallet and paid the pudgy, ice cream-scented bully, while Maggie reached across the counter and took hold of her dessert.

Wanting desperately to impress Bradley, she used extra caution in carrying the cardboard bowl full of the chocolaty dessert she had in her hands. Holding on tightly, she never took her eyes off of the sundae to guarantee it didn't tip or spill, all the while thinking, *Careful…*

She tiptoed back from the counter, turned, and *bam!* Smashing directly into Bradley, they were now standing chest to chest, the paper dish full of frozen dairy mashed flat between the two of them. Maggie gasped, timidly raising her eyes to his. Standing his ground, he reached up and flicked a whipped cream-covered almond from her eyebrow. Feeling the heat of his breath on her face made her tingly. She wished she could freeze this moment in time, minus the blob of ice cream wedged between them. Their body heat caused the ice cream to melt and slide down, landing on Bradley's shoe with a plop. "I am so sorry," she said.

Grabbing some napkins from the silver dispenser sitting on the counter, she started to blot the ice cream from his shirt, her strokes becoming slower and slower until the cleaning turned into more of a massage. She was mesmerized.

Noticing Mr. Wickham's glare, Bradley gently took her hand into his to stop the rubbing. "I'll take over from here," he said, brushing a large chunk from his shirt.

"Great job, Maggie Bug! I wanted to throw a dish of ice cream at him myself," Mr. Wickham shouted, his strange interpretation of the event destroying any romantic feelings she was feeling.

"Sorry, Mr. Wickham, I guess I just wasn't paying attention."

"I will remake your dessert, but this time I will take it to your table. Go sit down and try not to make another mess. And keep your hands off of that boy."

Embarrassed and feeling like a scolded child, she did as she was told. Bradley followed behind her, sucking on his strawberry malt, seemingly unscathed by the collision.

"I am sorry," Maggie apologized again. "In case you haven't noticed, I am a tad bit clumsy."

He let out one of his signature laughs that were genuine and flowed freely. "That's okay. It's just part of your charm."

Mr. Wickham came to the table and placed Maggie's desert in front of her, along with a pile of napkins. "I assume you'll need these," he said, before walking back to his post behind the counter.

Bradley asked, "So tell me about yourself. I have noticed you spend a lot of time with Sylvia. Is she a relative of yours?"

"Not officially. You see, my mother passed away when I was eleven and…"

"Oh, I am so sorry. I didn't know," he said, his words full of compassion.

"That's okay. I am sure it would be nice to have a mother, but I know God loved me so much, he gave me a replacement of sorts. Sylvia loves me as much as my own mother would. She may get me into trouble sometimes, but she really means well."

She went on to explain the wonderful relationships she had, when she suddenly realized she had talked for almost a half an hour, and Bradley had genuinely listened to every word.

"Sorry, I took up so much of your time."

"No, I enjoy listening to you. You just make me happy."

"I do?" she asked.

"Yes. Yes, you do."

He began saying something about the weather, but Maggie stopped listening, hypnotized by his moving lips. She thought, *They look so soft and kissable. I wonder how many women he has made out with. I bet he has starlets and mob boss daughters throwing themselves at him all the time.* Her insecurity was suddenly replaced with a hopeful idea. *Maybe he is bored with that kind of lifestyle and he wants someone a little more down to earth. Someone who will love him, take care of his house, and at night, run their fingers through his hair until he falls asleep.*

The long slurping sound he made as he finished off his malt brought her back to the conversation, just in time to hear him say, "I guess we should get going. I need to get you home before someone thinks you've been kidnapped."

"Kidnapped?" The word caused shivers to go up her spine, and it reminded her, she really didn't know anything about this boy other than he liked real fruit in his malts. She said, "Sure, but first, I need to say goodbye to Mr. Wickham." She excused herself and went to the counter. "Thanks for everything, Mr. Wickham. Just like I told Bradley, you have the best ice cream in town. It was delicious."

Stepping around the counter, he got very close to her and whispered, "Be careful with that boy. He looks shady to me, but then, no boy will ever be good enough for our Maggie Bug. If he says one cross word to you, I will tromp a mud hole in his backside."

"I appreciate that, sir." She threw her arms around him, and he held the embrace tightly. His words made her feel safe, but she hoped with all of her might that he was wrong about Bradley. Pulling a hand towel from his back pocket, he dabbed the tears that were pooling up in his eyes as they separated.

Changing the subject to restore his tough guy persona, he said, "Tell your daddy to get in here and get himself some ice cream therapy."

"You got it, sir."

Turning towards the door, she took in the view of the handsome Bradley, standing before her. His smile increased, the closer she got. *How in the world am I going to get my father's permission to marry a mobster?* she thought.

THE PLAN TAKES SHAPE

The biscuits were in the oven, and the sausage was sizzling as it browned in the skillet when her father came into the kitchen. "Morning, Maggie poo. How is my girl this morning?" He gave her a kiss on the cheek as she handed him a glass of cranberry juice.

"I am wonderful, Daddy," she replied, her heart full of joy.

"Did you have a good time at the movies last night with Sylvia?"

Maggie had hoped her father would have forgotten about her scheme, but since he brought it up, she had no choice but to continue the charade. "No need to tell you all the boring details about the movie, Daddy, because it was a flop. And if that wasn't bad enough, the popcorn was stale. But we made the best of it." Her father had already picked up the newspaper and sat down at the kitchen table. His shallow attention was her cue to change the subject without being obvious.

"Sylvia told me they have a new triple-chocolate, chunk, brownie mix at the market. I think I will run and pick one up and make us some brownies for dessert tonight. How does that sound to you?"

"I love brownies," he said, not lifting his eyes from the newspaper.

"Great. I will grab a box when I am out. Now, do you want four or five biscuits today?"

"I think I can go with five today since I had a salad for supper last night."

"Daddy, you cannot count the parsley in your meatloaf as salad. Maybe we should just start with four biscuits."

He let out a disgusted sigh, but his frustration left once Maggie served him the steaming pile of white carb-filled food. In a few bites, his plate was clean, and without Maggie's notice, he snuck another biscuit before giving her a kiss on the cheek as he headed out the door.

With her father out of the way, Maggie took the vacuum from the hall closet and began her weekly cleaning. She plugged the sweeper into the wall and flipped the switch. The loud roar of the motor drowned out all sound, but it was not loud enough to quite her thoughts of Bradley. She knew she should call Sylvia and update her on last night's date, but she just wanted to take a little more time basking in the glow of such a wonderful night before Sylvia came in like a bully and popped her happiness balloon.

That popping came sooner than she realized. Her tranquility and joy was interrupted by an intense pounding on the door. She turned the vacuum off and could see Sylvia peeking through the curtains in a slightly crouched position, her gun pulled, both hands firmly grasping the handle.

Well, I guess I can't avoid her any longer, she thought as she unlocked the door.

The moment Maggie turned the handle to release the lock, Sylvia reared back and crashed through the door, knocking Maggie off of her feet, sending her sprawling against the wall.

"I will blow your freaking head off! No one messes with my girl. Now show yourself you big coward!"

"Sylvia! Calm down. No one is here."

"Oh, the sissy saw me coming and took off, did he?" She ran to the back door and threw it open, jumping onto the small cement patio, pointing her gun to the right, then quickly to the left, itching to find a target to shoot at.

"Sylvia, no one is here, and no one was."

She dropped her gun to her side, totally disappointed she had no one to shoot. "I never heard from you, so I figured the bum was on to us. I just knew he had you tied up somewhere, hoping to get you to tell him everything we had uncovered. And knowing you like I do, I assumed you had spilled the beans pretty quickly. I was going to turn him into swiss cheese if he harmed one hair on your head."

"Sylvia, that is horrible! I can't believe you would even think like that."

"Wait a minute! You think I am dead all the time."

"Well, that is true." Maggie surrendered the point to her friend, knowing there were more important things they needed to discuss. She started adjusting the books on the coffee table in an attempt to delay the inevitable, but Sylvia's impatient foot tapping let her know it was time to spill the beans. "I have been thinking, maybe…maybe we…maybe we have jumped to conclusions." She swallowed hard, then continued. "What if Bradley is really just a nice guy who was forced into this life of crime because of circumstances we know nothing about? Maybe his heart really isn't in it. Maybe he is the victim in this scenario. Maybe he is the one that needs to be rescued!"

"Oh, no!" Sylvia plopped down into the wooden kitchen chair, elbows on the table, head in her hands. "I knew it," she said. "That parasite has gotten under your skin." She turned and looked up at Maggie, "Gee wiz, girl! That skunk used the oldest trick in the book to distract you. Charm. It is one of the techniques used by male-brainwashing experts everywhere." Sylvia leaned closer to Maggie to emphasis her point, "It is a fact, when a man works up all of his machismo, it causes him to release extra pheromones. Those pheromones attract and confuse the female. Once he intoxicates you with his manly chemicals, he's got cha'!"

Maggie listened intently to her much more experienced partner before asking, "But I was just thinking—"

"Hold on!" Sylvia interrupted. "Do you hear that sucking sound?" She cupped her hand around her ear. "That sound, my dear, is you getting sucked into his web."

Maggie sat down at the table, her heart and mind going in two different directions.

Sylvia continued the lesson, "Listen to me. Tomorrow you will find out what Mr. Bradley, the bad guy, is all about. When you see the harm and heartache he has caused, you will be thankful I was here to protect you. Shake this off. The heart is fickle and can't be trusted. Just like Bradley. Okay?"

Maggie processed Sylvia's council for a moment then sadly said, "I appreciate that you are so willing to share all of your life's wisdom with me. Like you said, I need to just shake this off and complete our mission."

"That's my girl." Sylvia gave her a playful punch in the arm and continued, "Now, while you were cavorting with the enemy, I was thinking about how we need to get old lady Jensen out of her house and stash her safely out of harm's way, so we can set up a sting and catch her lousy grandson. I thought I would give her a call and invite her to go with me to play bingo. No one would ever think to look for her there."

Sylvia took the telephone headset from the phone hanging on the wall, and pulled a slip of paper from the pocket of her flowered cotton frock. Dialing the number that was scribbled on the paper, she impatiently twirled the cord on the phone while she waited for the elderly woman to answer. After several rings, she began to move the phone from her ear to place it back on the receiver when she heard a feeble voice speaking on the other end, "Hello?"

"Hello, Mrs. Jensen?"

"Hello, is there anyone there?"

Sylvia spoke louder, "Hello, Mrs. Jensen, this is Sylvia Coy."

"I'm sorry, honey, I don't know any boy."

"I said Coy!" Sylvia shouted into the phone, pronouncing each word slowly and distinctly. "I. Am. Sylvia Coy!"

"Oh, I'm sorry. I don't hear so well, anymore. Let me try turning up my hearing aid." There was a brief pause before she came back on the line. "Okay, yes. I remember you, Sylvia Coy. You are the home wrecker that destroyed my best friend Lucy's marriage, many years ago."

"Excuse me?" Sylvia replied, her voice suddenly tense with irritation.

"I specifically remember how you flaunted yourself in front of Lucy's husband, Carl, until he surrendered to your charms. I also remember thinking, "Why in the world is he demanding his wife keep you as their housekeeper when all you ever did was sit and watch soap operas all day." The words poured out, the memories as clear as if the incident happened the day before. She continued, "It all made sense when he dumped Lucy, so he could go shack up with you in your den of iniquity."

Sylvia was fiercely angry but contained herself, knowing she had to remain calm or she could ruin the whole plan. She looked to Maggie for reassurance and was met with a thumbs-up and a smile from her oblivious partner.

She exhaled deeply, reminding herself that if she didn't take the bus over to this woman's house and drag her outside by her hair and demand an apology, there would be wonderful accolades in her future from her community for saving the woman that she herself couldn't stand. She forced a smile to sweeten her words. "Now, darling, I never wrecked their home. It was wrecked long before I came along, but hey, that is the past and you know what Father Ray says, we need to forgive and move on. How about we start fresh? Funny thing is, I was just thinking the other day how I would love to spend some time with you, just being buddies, when I opened the newspaper and fate offered me an opportunity to do just that. Tomorrow at the Legion, they are hosting a bingo marathon, and I was wondering if you would like to go with me?" She rolled her eyes, crossed her fingers, and said in a strained voice, "Just like old friends."

Mrs. Jensen skipped over Sylvia's invite. She had years' worth of pent up frustration she wanted to get out and was happy to get this opportunity. She continued her rant. "I always wondered what Carl saw in you. I mean, you being so fat and all."

Sylvia's blood pressure shot up, her face turning red in anger. "Oh no, you didn't. Did you just call me fat?"

"Well yes, dear, I did. Chunky, obese, fluffy, whatever you want to hear. That's what I said."

Sylvia began to huff and puff, sweat already beginning to form on her brow. She took another deep breath, but instead of a relaxing exhale, she used the air in her fully expanded lungs to start yelling.

"Well, tootsie, while we are on the subject of appearance, have you looked in a mirror lately, you decrepit old fart! You have more wrinkles than an elephant. Your hair looks like it was done by a blind man wearing mittens, and you smell like mothballs! Wait!" She paused a momentary, dramatic pause, setting up her perfectly designed insult. "Do you hear that ringing?" Another suspenseful pause was followed by, "It's a call for you. It's the 1800s, and they want their schoolmarm outfits back!" Not about to stop now, she added, "Let me, the expert, give you a little bit of knowledge. Meat is for the man, and bones are for the dogs. Men like a woman with some meat on them, and Carl was one of those kind of guys. He came to my arms because he loved to lay his head on my big ample breasts, something you wouldn't know anything about, you old bag of bones!"

There was a click on the phone line as Mrs. Jensen ended the call abruptly.

Sylvia said into the receiver, "Hello? Hello? Mrs. Jensen, are you there?"

She stared into the phone before turning around and hanging up. "If Bradley doesn't kill her, I'm going to," she said to Maggie.

"What in the world happened?"

"She said I was fat. She also called me a home wrecker, but that part is kind of true, so I am not really offended at that. But she crossed a line with the fat comment."

Maggie tried to calm Sylvia, who was now pacing the kitchen like a caged animal. "Old lady Jensen doesn't realize you are not fat, you are just big boned. She's just jealous because you are voluptuous and she isn't."

Sylvia contemplated the comment then said, "You know what? I think you are right. I dated an artist once who told me I was Rubenesque, and there were paintings in some of the greatest museums in the world of naked women who were built just like me." She stood taller and stuck out her breasts in pride, trying to catch a glimpse of her reflection in the glass of the back door. "That old cuss is just jealous of this knockout body of mine. I wouldn't be surprised if she really had the hots for Carl herself, and the fact that I stole him first has stuck in her craw all of these years." She sat back down at the table, her frown now replaced by a smug grin. "Good thing you talked me down because I had decided I wasn't going to save her sorry life. Good riddance, if you ask me. But after this new revelation, I think we should go ahead and protect her scrawny butt. That will totally prove to her I am as wonderful on the inside as I am on the outside."

Maggie sighed in relief before asking, "So what do we do next?"

Sylvia went into the entryway, where she had thrown her jacket across a chair. Reaching into the pocket, she pulled out a large piece of paper that was neatly rolled into a tube. She returned to the kitchen, unrolled the paper across the table, set the salt shaker on one corner to hold it down, and the butter dish on the opposite side to prevent the paper from curling back into its circular shape. "I spent all of yesterday creating this drawing of old lady Jensen's property."

Maggie looked intently, trying to find something familiar in the drawing but was getting distracted by Sylvia's unique artwork. She asked, "What is this blue blob beside this green blob?"

Unable to really tell what the nondescript item was she had drawn, Sylvia leaned in and out until a memory was sparked. "Umm, oh yes! That is the birdbath under the old oak tree on the Cochran property, next door."

Maggie leaned in to get a better look, but pulled back after identifying the same two colorful blobs she originally saw. She continued to question. "And what is this red-and-yellow square on the corner of the page?"

"That is the restaurant down the street from her house. You know? Miller's Grill. They have the best tenderloins I ever ate."

"What does that have to do with Mrs. Jensen?"

"Nothing, but I thought we might need a place to eat lunch after our stakeout."

Spending the best part of an hour going over the drawing and discussing their plan. Sylvia finally stood up, "Okay, Mags. We can do this. We are smart women."

Maggie, who was nervously twirling her hair, said "I am just concerned that Daddy is going to be very angry with me for putting myself in harm's way."

"Are you kidding me?" Sylvia said. "When he sees his baby girl on TV getting an award from the mayor for bravery, he will be beaming with pride. All the guys at the factory will shake his hand and tell him what a great job he did in raising such a wonderful daughter."

Maggie smiled, imagining her father's pleasure and pride. Sylvia did not let her stay in that happy place for very long. She said, "Next thing on our agenda, what time are you picking me up tomorrow? We need to allow ourselves time to get into place before the 'attempted massacre' begins. I was thinking—" She stopped speaking, realizing the absence of interaction from Maggie. "Mags, you did get tomorrow off, didn't you?"

Maggie's eyes got wide, and she began shaking her head, emphatically no. "There is no way! I can't lie to Mr. Gene. He was a Marine, and he was trained to tell if someone was lying. He will read right through me."

"Quit freaking out. All you have to do is tell him you have diarrhea or female problems. Trust me. No man wants the details of either of those maladies."

Maggie's nerves were getting the best of her. She went to the sink and ran a dishcloth under the cold water, rang it out, and put it on her forehead. "I am out. I can't do it. I thought I could, but now I know…"

Sylvia had already dialed the diner and shoved the phone up to Maggie's ear.

Maggie dropped the cloth and took hold of the receiver. She was frozen in place when Mr. Gene answered.

Sylvia snapped her fingers, bringing Maggie back to earth.

"Hello, Mr. Gene, this is Maggie. I needed to call you and let you know, I think I have the stomach flu. I have spent most of the morning in the bathroom, and I am sure I will be there for the next twenty-four hours. Don't worry about me because I am staying hydrated and getting plenty of rest."

There was silence on Maggie's end of the conversation, and Sylvia knew Mr. Gene had begun his questioning. She ran around and stood directly in front of Maggie and flexed her muscles as if she was an Olympic bodybuilder. "Stay strong," she whispered.

Maggie nodded in agreement. "No, Mr. Gene, this has nothing to do with any boy. I do need to hang up now because I think I am going to throw up." She quickly ended the call by slamming the receiver back on its base and looked at Sylvia. "I wasn't lying about the throwing up part." She sat back in the chair and put the wet cloth back on her forehead as Sylvia began fanning her with a placemat from the table.

Sylvia said, "Great job, kid!" She put down the mat and said, "Now, all of this crime fighting has made me hungry, and I smelled biscuits and gravy when I came in. Detective work burns an awful lot of calories, and we don't want to pass out from low blood sugar while chasing down a perp. Since we are on the beat tomorrow, we better do some carb loading today." She grabbed a plate from the cabinet. "Got any apple butter to go with these biscuits?" she asked.

DRESSING FOR THE BIG EVENT

THE BIG DAY had arrived. Maggie woke up exhausted, her mind running in circles all night. "I'll be glad when this is over cause it sure is messin' with my sleep. No wonder law enforcement people always seem so serious. They're just tired."

She got out of bed and picked a bright-yellow top then combined it with a pair of crumpled khakis as her outfit for the day. To tame the wrinkles that covered her pants, she turned on the faucet in the bathroom and let the water run into her hands. She rubbed her wet hands up and down her pant legs, hoping the moisture would encourage the wrinkles to release their grip.

The tiny creases were being very stubborn, so an increase of "liquid persuasion" was needed. She slipped the pants off and laid them across the bathroom counter. Cupping her hands, the water filled up her rounded palms. Holding all she could, she threw the small puddle of liquid onto the pants, drowning out the unsightly wrinkles.

Satisfied with her "ironing" job, she grabbed the belt loops and stepped into the dripping wet pants and secured them. She took the brush from the vanity and pulled it through her hair until she had tamed her locks into a ponytail then secured it with an elastic band high upon the back of her head.

A last look in the mirror completed her grooming, so she headed downstairs where she found the kitchen completely dark. Ordinarily, she hated it when her father had to work on the weekends, but this specific Saturday, she was grateful he was busy and unable to ask any questions.

She grabbed a powdered sugar doughnut from a bag in the kitchen cabinet and a can of Dr. Pepper before pulling a note from her back pocket Sylvia had given her the night before. Written in her distinctive handwriting were the following words: Vaseline, rope, bobby pins, iPod, Oreo's, Cheetos, two liter of Dr. Pepper. All items she thought would be vital to a successful stakeout. Maggie never questioned any of Sylvia's requests but instead gathered them together and shoved them into a tote, carrying them out to her car.

After the bag was secured in the backseat, she put the keys in the ignition, but before she pulled out of the drive, she closed her eyes, folded her hands, and began to pray, "God, please be with us today as we are doing a good work. Please keep us safe and let good triumph over evil. Please do not let Sylvia shoot anyone, and please let her be alive when I knock on her door. Thank you for your grace and protection. Oh, and one more thing. Let Bradley change his ways while he is in jail for the crime he is about to commit. Amen."

The drive to Sylvia's seemed to be a short one with all of the adrenaline Maggie had coursing through her veins, which only added to the anxiety she felt once she had arrived and was standing on her porch. "Please don't be dead, please don't be dead, please don't be dead," she chanted under her breath as she knocked on the door.

Sylvia threw open the door and chuckled, "Worried I was dead?"

Maggie was frozen in place, not because Sylvia was alive, but because her appearance was anything but normal. "You look like a ninja shrub!" Maggie exclaimed. "This is your best creation yet!"

Sylvia stepped back and did a few turns as if she was a runway model in Milan, proud to show off her new camouflaged ensemble, which consisted of material in every shade of gray and green cut into random shapes and sown onto a gray jogging suit. Her fancy church hat had been sacrificed to complete the look, the original, silk flowers were removed from the band and replaced with leaves and dead branches from her yard that were stitched tightly to the felt with the only thing sturdy enough to hold the heavy items—a red yarn.

Finishing off her disguise, several shades and varieties of makeup had been combined in a bowl, creating a mud-colored masque which she had smeared all over her face. The gloppy product had not worked down into her wrinkly crevices so whenever she changed her facial expressions, little white lines appeared amidst the murky face cream, emphasizing her emotions. She also failed to apply any of the makeup to her ears, so they appeared to glow as they stuck out of the side of her head.

"Maggie, were you aware that we were going to do a stakeout?"

"Yes, ma'am." she said, proudly.

"When you are on a stakeout, you are not to be seen, right?"

Maggie was not sure where the questioning was going, but she had a feeling she was about to be chastised.

"Why don't you just stick a spotlight on top of your head? I mean a yellow shirt for goodness sake?"

Maggie looked down at her outfit self-consciously then realized what her friend meant.

"You look like a walking safety cone from a construction site! Come on, girl, I will get you fixed up." Sylvia grabbed Maggie by her hand and led her into the bedroom.

She opened her closet and began rummaging through it. "No. No. No," stating her displeasure with each garment, throwing them into a pile onto the bed. Clothes were flying from every direction until she came to a garment which was wrapped in plastic, the name of the local dress boutique stamped on the protective covering.

Sylvia slowly pulled the dress out from the closet and gently lifted it as if it was a museum artifact. Puzzled, Maggie looked closely at the bright-blue dress covered in sequins, the price tag still attached to it.

"I am glad I saw this. I wanted to tell you about it, but I kept forgetting." Sylvia said, her voice becoming low and very serious. "This is my funeral dress."

"Sylvia!" Maggie exclaimed.

"You have to listen because that no good son of mine never does. I have tried to explain my burial plans to him on several occasions, and he just blows me off. That is why I am depending on you. Someday, far, far away, I will die and be in need of a funeral. Being the fashionista that I am, I refuse to be buried in some god-awful outfit that boy of mine would pick out. Knowing him and his lack of fashion sense that he got from his father, he would probably bury me in something orange, knowing full good and well, that color washes me out and makes me look like I have dark circles under my eyes." Admiringly, she ran her hand gently across the plastic before continuing, "So, last fall, I was shopping, and I saw this dress in the window of Einbender's Dress Boutique. I knew at that moment, I was going to be buried in that dress. I marched right into the store and put it on layaway. I also purchased shoes and a handbag and had them dyed to match the dress. They are in the bag on the floor of the closet marked "funeral accessories." In it are also a ring, clip-on earrings, and false eyelashes. Make sure I look good. And remember, I refuse to wear a brassiere for all of eternity, so no bra!"

Maggie had tears in her eyes, and Sylvia noticed. "Suck it up, kid. I ain't goin' nowhere for a long time. I just needed someone I trusted to know my last wishes. Now, we got to get you into something dark. Oh, I know." Sylvia gently hung the dress back into the closet before pulling a large, black smock from a box on the closet floor.

"I used to wear this when I was a shampoo girl," she said, slipping it over the still grieving Maggie's head. It was six sizes too big and hanging off one of her shoulders.

"Hmm," Sylvia contemplated. She went to the kitchen pantry and grabbed a spool of twine and her kitchen shears. Returning to Maggie, she reached her arms around her and pulled the twine around her tiny waist. "Gee wiz, girl! You could use a cupcake or something," Sylvia remarked, as she held up the short length of twine that had measured Maggie's mid-section. She folded the cordage, doubled the length, then lopped it off with the shears.

She reached around Maggie's waist again, but this time she pulled the twine tightly around her, tying it in a small, double knot in the location of her belly button.

Maggie walked over and looked at her reflection in the mirror. "I look like a baggy, black snowman."

"Perfect! Now for the pants." Sylvia went to the bed and pulled a box from underneath. Inside the container was a pile of neatly folded men's clothing.

"These were husband number seven's. He was long and lean, like you," Sylvia said before pulling out a pair of trousers. "Slip them on."

Maggie removed her still slightly-damp khakis before wrestling the big, black tent-like covering she was already wearing into a pile of material under one arm. Using her free hand to take hold of the waistband on the huge pair of men's pants, she stepped into them and hopped up and down until she had them in the proper location around her midsection. One last adjustment was made then she let them go. They immediately dropped straight to her feet in a heap.

"No need for panic, we can fix those also," Sylvia said. "Problem is not with the clothes, it is your lack of hips. Once we get through this, we really should start talking about your diet."

She took another length of twine and threaded it through the loop of the pants, gave it a good yank to make it snug, then tied it in a double knot as well. She stepped back to admire her handiwork. "Give us some movement," she encouraged Maggie.

Maggie moved her head slightly, and the pants slowly began creeping over her hips, but this time she grabbed them before they hit the ground.

Sylvia took her sewing kit from the top shelf of the closet and opened it before setting it on the bed. Stepping closer to her "model," she yanked the baggy pants up with such determination, Maggie had to take a moment to remove the wedgie it caused. Rolling the extra material until she formed a crease, Sylvia shoved a safety pin through the wad of cloth, creating a makeshift seam.

It did not take her long to use all of the safety pins she had in her kit, so she had no choice but to complete the job with straight pins. Warning Maggie, she said, "You will have to be careful when sitting. As long as you pay attention, you shouldn't lose any blood."

Once the alterations were complete, she reached into her underwear drawer and pulled out a black, nylon stocking. "Keep this in your pocket in case of emergency. You never know when you may have to hide your identity."

Sylvia turned Maggie back towards the mirror, placing her arm around her friend. "How amazing do we look?"

Sylvia was smiling, glowing ear to glowing ear, while Maggie's face was showing regret.

"Can you imagine the surprise on Bradley's face when we jump out and ruin his plan?" Sylvia threw her head back and laughed. "I can't wait to go kick some mobster butt."

As they headed to the door, Maggie's pants began to slide. She grabbed them and yelped, a straight pin pricking her index finger. "I'm already wounded!"

"Keep moving, tootsie," Sylvia said. "You will be just fine. No one has ever died from a pin prick. Well, maybe they have, but it is rare. Just spit on it. God put natural enzymes in saliva, and those enzymes act as natural antibiotics. That is why dogs don't need tetanus shots. They just lick everything."

There was just enough logic in that statement that Maggie didn't question it. Rather, she puddled up some saliva in her mouth, puckered up, and spit it onto the small bead of blood that had formed on her finger.

THE STAKEOUT

Maggie slowed down in an attempt to find a discreet place to park a block away from Mrs. Jensen's house. As usual, her aim was off, and she went up over the cement edging. Quickly yanking on the steering wheel, she came down safely against the curb. "Perfect," she said.

Sylvia was used to the abrupt stops, so no comment was necessary. Instead, she began telling her partner the plan. "Okay, I need you to follow me, because I know what I'm doing. I'm like a Navy Seal. I have snuck in and out of many houses, unnoticed by some the most observant wives."

Maggie agreed, "I'm glad you're in charge because I can't even sneak down to the kitchen for a cookie without waking my father. I remember one time I was tiptoeing down the hallway…"

Sylvia, deaf to Maggie's story, declared, "Here we go. No turning back. Let's kick butt and take names!" Maggie watched as Sylvia threw open the car door, ran across the sidewalk, jumped a chain-link fence, got down on her hands and knees, and crawled behind a shed for cover.

"Boy, that woman can really move," Maggie said out loud. She stepped out of her car then pressed the remote control to lock the doors. After a reassuring click to confirm the car was safe and sound, she began following Sylvia's path.

She skipped across the sidewalk and ran up to the fence but stopped short. She leaned against the chain link and measured the height, comparing it to the length of her legs. She backed up and ran towards it but stopped again. "There is no way I am going to get over that fence without breaking an arm or leg."

A survey of the property revealed a gate at the side of the yard, so she jogged over to it, lifted the gate latch, and entered into the yard. Gently, she closed the gate, moving very slowly, careful to avoid making any noise. The pride she took in her prowess was quickly replaced with curiosity as a low, fierce growl could be heard right behind her. Turning ever so slowly, she stood three feet from a huge, black-and-brown, Shepherd-mixed dog. It was crouched down, every muscle in its body on high alert. With drool dripping from his yellow, clenched teeth, it started creeping toward her.

"Hi, puppy. Good puppy. Nice puppy?" she said, her voice barely above a whisper. "It's okay. I am nice. I like doggies." Maggie reached out to pat the head of the rabid-looking fur ball with teeth. He snapped his mouth shut, barely missing her fingers.

"Heeelp!" Maggie screamed. Fearing for her life, she took off running toward Sylvia. She was only able to take two quick steps before her oversized outfit aided the dog in his attack, her pants sliding to her thighs, causing her to stumble. With laser-like precision, the maniac mongrel clamped down, catching Maggie's pants between its teeth.

He planted his feet and leaned back, pulling Maggie's feet out from under her. With all of his strength, he shook his head violently from side-to-side, slipping the baggy britches from her small frame without much hindrance.

As he whipped the pants from side to side in a sign of victory, she lay in the grass whimpering, her red-and-white polka-dot undies shining in the sun.

Preparing herself for the inevitability of becoming a chew toy, she curled into a ball. The sound of footsteps approaching could barely be heard through her sniveling. She peaked over her arm she had covering her face and saw her hero. Like a ninja swinging a sword, she watched as Sylvia grabbed one of the tree limbs from her hat and took a swing. The blow connected to the top of dog's head. He let out a confused yelp, causing it to drop Maggie's pants.

A second whack was not necessary for the canine to realize it had met its match. Retreating under the front porch of the house for safety, it gave Sylvia enough time to help Maggie to her feet. She picked up the pants before leading her to the back side of the shed.

"Did I tell you to follow me?" Sylvia said, sternly.

"Yes," Maggie replied sheepishly.

"Did you think I was just saying that because I love the sound of my own voice so much I use words for no good reason?"

"Maybe. Sometimes."

"Real funny. Now pay attention. First, we have to fix these." She held up Maggie's pants with the newly-torn hole in the seat. With great precision, she took a pin from the waistband of the men's-trousers-turned-spy-suit, pulled the hole closed, and stuck the metal fastener through it. She shoved them back in Maggie's face. "Good as new. Put them back on."

Maggie did just as she was told, but once the pants were in place, it was pretty obvious to them both that the safety pin was not enough to repair the gaping hole the dog had left in the seat. Quick thinking, Sylvia bent down and grabbed a handful of dirt. Grabbing Maggie by the shoulder, she spun her around, bent her over, then rubbed soil all over the neon-colored underwear that was peeking through the hole.

Maggie looked over her shoulder and could still see her undergarment. "Maybe, I could go home and change really quick."

"You can't even tell." Sylvia lied, crossing her fingers in hopes the gesture would disqualify the fib. "Time is of the essence. Look at me"—she took Maggie's face in her hands—"Old lady Jensen needs us, and even though she's a mean old beast, we have to save her life. Now let's get on with this."

"Promise me Bradley won't see my po po," Maggie said.

"Promise. Now follow me."

Sneaking towards Mrs. Jensen's house, this time with Maggie close behind, they hid behind trees, ducked behind bushes, and tiptoed through yards until they had finally reached the Jensen's garage. Maggie's nerves were beginning to get the best of her.

"Sylvia, we've made a big mistake. We need to call the police right now. We are in way over our heads. We are not law enforcement." Maggie leaned against the building to try and steady her trembling. "Oh, and one more thing. I don't want to die."

"Get yourself under control. We are as qualified as most of the law enforcement in this town. Actually, I would say we are more qualified because no one suspects us of being as brilliant as we obviously are."

She turned, grabbed Maggie by the shoulders, and looked her in the eyes. "You need to know a few things. First, I am not about to do anything to get myself thrown in prison, someone like me would be real popular in a place like that. Second, even though I have already purchased my funeral dress, I'm not about to die today because I have a hair appointment Monday, and I'm not going to heaven until my hair looks nice. And lastly, I would never, ever, ever, let anything happen to you."

Maggie was touched by her friend's statement. Deep down she knew she would really protect her. "I promise you, we can do this," Sylvia said. That was enough to energize Maggie.

"If you are sure, then I am sure," Maggie said, feebly.

Sylvia nodded in agreement and said, "We got this."

A high-five sealed their pact, but their celebrating was cut short by the sound of an approaching vehicle. Sylvia held her finger to her lips. "Shhh." She peeked around the side of the garage but turned back to process what she just saw.

"There must be fifteen cars parked in front of her house. Why in the world would a person want that many witnesses?" Sylvia began pacing and chastising herself for not knowing the answer to her own question immediately. "Come on, woman, think! Why would a criminal want that many people in a location where he was about to blow somebody up? Hmm, think, think, th…wait! I got it! Bradley is going to do this hit like one of those murder-mystery dinner theaters. I bet you he will shut off the power so when he puts the old crank out of her misery, no one will see who did it. Then when the lights come back on, there will be chaos. Everyone will be blaming each other for the crime, and while they are fighting amongst themselves, that lowlife will sneak out, unnoticed. Right out the back door, I bet. I must say, he thinks he is smart, but it's pretty obvious I am smarter than he is." She smiled proudly.

Maggie was thoroughly impressed with her partner. "Wow, Sylvia! That is amazing. I can't wait to get in front of the news cameras and tell everyone how you figured out every detail of this crime. I am lucky to even be here with you."

"I know, right? I have always had a devious mind. I guess it is just a blessing from the Lord that I use my powers for good and not evil," she said, piously.

The sound of a vehicle coming closer caused Sylvia to turn and look again, "Oh, no! It's Bradley in old lady Jensen's car. He will see us!"

A shove from Sylvia knocked unsuspecting Maggie off her feet. Landing in some large bushes, Sylvia plopped right beside her after completing a very impressive swan dive.

Victorious in their attempt to be completely hidden from sight, a new problem immediately arose. The bushes that were providing their coverage were very mature barberry bushes, completely covered in thorns. Maggie was trying hard not to cry, but the sound that came out of her tightly-closed lips sounded a lot like a kitten that was being squeezed. Sylvia clamped her hand over the mouth of her friend to muffle her whimper. Tears welled up in Maggie's eyes, taking no time at all to spill over and run down her cheeks.

The car drove past the shrubs full of women and pulled into the driveway. Sylvia released her grip from Maggie's mouth, and they climbed from the bushes, looking as if they had been attacked by a mob of angry felines. Their clothing was torn, and the tiny scratches that covered the bodies were already seeping blood.

"Maggie," Sylvia whispered and pointed towards Mrs. Jensen's house, "look at the spider drawing the fly into his web."

She felt a tickle and looked down to see a trail of blood trickling down her hand. "Well, my first war wound. These scars will be impressive when I retell this story."

Maggie on the other hand was a bit more worried about possible infection. "You wouldn't have any antibiotic ointment would you?" she quietly asked Sylvia.

"Sure. I have some in my pocket-sized first aid kit."

"Really?"

"No! Crime fighters do not carry first aid kits! What do you think we are? A couple of sissies?" She reached down her top and pulled a Kleenex from her bra. "Here, use this to mop up the blood. And don't forget to spit on it first."

As Maggie moistened the tissue before blotting the tiny red lines on her arms, she looked over Sylvia's shoulder and watched Bradley open the car door before carefully helping his feeble grandmother from the vehicle.

Maggie stopped looking, her heart saddened by what she just witnessed. "The stinker opened the door for her, just like he did for me. Maybe I was wrong. Maybe you can be a gentleman and still be evil to the core," she said, sadly.

SOMETHING IS NOT LINING UP

MAGGIE LEANED BACK against the garage and put her index and middle finger on the side of neck, taking note of her racing pulse. Adding the irregular heartbeat to her shallow breathing confirmed her complete panic state. Needing moral support, she turned to her partner in crime for comfort only to find she had already relocated herself at the Jensen's privacy fence that surrounded the backyard. She watched as Sylvia pulled and tugged on each board, stopping long enough to peek through the cracks at the gathering crowd on the other side.

"The backyard is full of very nicely-dressed people. I don't see the victim-to-be yet, so we need to hustle and get in place," Sylvia said, breathlessly, as Maggie finally got into place. "Don't just stand there shaking like a wet cat. Find a loose board. We need to get into this backyard now or it is going to be too late!"

Maggie was grabbing and shaking boards when she heard a *snap*. Sylvia had pulled a board loose. Wasting no time, the ladies quickly grabbed the next board, using the newly opened space to gain leverage. The second board popped off with very little effort.

"Bradley and his mob friends are in for the surprise of their lives. I wish I had a camera to get a picture of their expressions," Sylvia said, her intensity making her sound a little demented. The sweat that was now rolling down her chubby face was causing her brown camo paint to slide from her cheeks onto the collar of her homemade camouflaged shirt.

Focused on her task, Sylvia said, "I think if you grab the top of this board and pull it out, I can slide my fingers into the crack and get a better grip."

Maggie stood on her tiptoes and firmly grabbed the top of the plank as she was told.

"Okay," Sylvia whispered, "I want you to pull as hard as you can on three. One, two, three!"

Maggie yanked on the board with all of her might, and it popped loose, sending her stumbling backward, arms and legs flailing, trying desperately to find something to grasp a hold of. Her feet, unable to keep up with gravity's pull, lost their position and sent her crashing to the ground with such force, the air left her lungs in a groan.

Sylvia never saw the fall. She already had her head, neck, and one shoulder shoved through the newly created gap in the wooden privacy fence. Wiggling to the left then to the right, she pulled out of the slot, took a better look, then came at it from a different angle. Shoving her arm and shoulder through the hole, she used her free hand to smash her breasts in an attempt to make them flatter. No luck there.

Wiping the sweat from her brow, it hit her! Her mud makeup would be the perfect lubricant. She wiped the brown, creamy product from her forehead and smeared it all over her chest, and the slimy concoction she removed from her cheeks was wiped across her protruding belly. She stepped back, eyeballed the opening, then lunged at the slot. One good grunt and she popped through the fence. Maggie watched as Sylvia was "birthed" through the wooden canal. *Well, if she can do it, I can do it,* Maggie thought.

She put her head through the slats, wanting to make sure her landing spot was free from wild animals, but nothing could have prepared her for what she was about to see. Sylvia reach into the pants of her jogging suit and pulled out her revolver like an old west gunslinger, firing a warning shot into the air before giving the command, "Everybody, freeze!"

The nicely-dressed guests began screaming. Some dove under the tables to find safety; some ran for the exits, and one aristocratic-looking woman grabbed her chest and fainted. Sylvia looked around the beautifully decorated yard full of white, linen-covered chairs that surrounded large, strategically arranged tables. Beautiful bouquets of tulips, daffodils, and hyacinths tucked in crystal vases sat in the middle of each table, with fine china, and shiny silverware completing the stunning place settings.

On the patio were long buffet tables covered with mountains of food on silver trays. A man in a white jacket and a chef's hat had been slicing pieces from a huge hunk of prime rib but fled out of the gate the moment bullets started to fly.

An archway, covered in silver balloons, framed the table where a three-tiered cake decorated with tiny pink rosebuds rested. Next to the cake was a silver fountain full of a pink, frothy liquid that poured over two tiers before gathering into a shiny bowl at the bottom.

Sylvia looked around for her back up and found Maggie lying on the ground, her hands covering her head, praying, "Please, God, forgive Sylvia. I think she has dementia."

Sylvia gave the command, "Now is not the best time for praying. I think that could have been done before we broke in." She gave Maggie a little nudge with her foot to motivate her to get into an upright position.

At that moment, Bradley stepped onto the patio with Mrs. Jensen's arm wrapped around him. He turned to watch the old lady's expression as he yelled, "Surprise!" Mrs. Jensen let out a squeal of excitement, thrilled she had just been escorted to her own surprise party. He began applauding, but his handclaps became quieter and slower as he noticed there was no participation on behalf of the other guests. He turned his gaze from his grandmother, looking from one end of the yard to the other. He saw the balloons blowing in the cool spring breeze, but the faint sound of a woman crying and people lying on the ground made him realize something had went terribly wrong.

Sylvia came running towards him, revolver pointing in the air. She grabbed Mrs. Jensen by the arm and yanked her away from Bradley. "We have saved your life!" she declared.

Pulling a set of shiny handcuffs from her sock, she reached behind herself to give the restraining device to Maggie, not taking her eyes or aim off of Bradley. "Here, Maggie, take these and lock up that beast." Getting no response, she repeated her request, dangling the cuffs to get her partner's attention. "Maggie, take these." The jingling cuffs hung heavily from Sylvia's fingers until she impatiently turned to find out what was causing the delay. She panned the crowd, finding her partner, thirty yards away, hiding behind the punch fountain. "Get over here," Sylvia scolded her.

Hesitantly, she came out of hiding. "Hello, everyone," she said coyly, giving a nod and a wave to the people she passed as she headed towards Sylvia. "Beautiful day out here, isn't it?" She smiled at a middle-aged woman who was frozen in place, still holding a piece of shrimp in mid-bite. "What a lovely dress. Did you get that at Einbenders? You know, my friend Sylvia, she is the one up there with the gun, she has the most beautiful funeral dress she bought from there. Just today, she—"

"Maggie!" Sylvia jingled the handcuffs to bring Maggie back to task. "Oh, excuse me," she said to the lady, whose hands were now shaking so bad, the shrimp shook loose and dropped on the ground. Maggie picked it up, blew the grass clipping off of it, and placed it gently in the shocked female's hand. "There ya' go. Sylvia needs me up front but maybe we could talk later." Tripping over an abandoned clutch before finally reaching the front of the crowd, she took the cuffs from Sylvia and walked over to Bradley.

He was frozen in place; his eyes locked on Sylvia's gun that was pointed directly at him. Maggie's hands were shaking and sweat had formed on her upper lip, and the moment she took hold of his hand, her face flushed. As the handcuffs closed on his wrist, a plump gray-haired man in a navy-blue suit jumped out from behind a bush. "Someone stop that lunatic!"

Sylvia spun around and pointed her gun directly at the old man's crotch, saying through gritted teeth, "I am a perfect shot with this thing. If you ever want to pee standing up again, you will shut your mouth. I don't know if you are part of this 'hit' or not, but I think you should know, we are not afraid of your kind, so back off, Jacko!"

The stunned man went weak in the knees and stumbled backwards, flopping down in a chair. Sylvia turned the gun back towards Bradley then declared to the crowd, "Folks, I am sorry to inform you, but this ain't no party. This man standing before you is a mobster."

"Oh, we are having lobster?" Mrs. Jensen asked, clapping with excitement.

Sylvia stomped her foot in disgust. "I said mobster, you old bat! Mob, not lob!"

"What are we eating then if we are not having lobster?" Mrs. Jensen asked.

Sylvia, unaware she was using her weapon as a pointer, told Maggie, "Take that crazy old woman to the buffet table and get her something to eat. Go ahead and fix me a plate while you are there. I am going to be starving by the time the cops get here." Each time she gave a direction, the crowd gasped in fear of getting shot by pure accident.

Maggie, relieved to get away from the gun, reached out and took Mrs. Jensen by the arm, "Let's get you something to eat."

Mrs. Jensen, straining to hear, said, "Pete? No, that is my grandson, Bradley, not Pete." Maggie rolled her eyes, gently leading the guest of honor to the tables piled with the still uneaten food.

Sylvia yelled to Maggie, "Be sure and get me a piece of cake with a rose on it. I love that extra frosting. Well, unless it is that yucky whipped icing. If that is the case, I don't even want cake, and whoever made it should be sued for ruining a perfectly beautiful cake by putting that fake stuff on it."

Bradley, keenly aware of her distraction, slowly began sliding his foot backward in an attempt to make an escape. Sylvia spun around and aimed her gun at him, bringing another collective gasp from the crowd. Bradley lifted his shackled hands in front of his face and whimpered, "Please don't shoot me. I am not a mobster. Maggie, tell her." Not a word was uttered from his chosen character witness. She just continued walking Mrs. Jensen towards the food, pretending to not hear his pleas.

"Shut up, punk," Sylvia demanded. "Maggie and I have been doing surveillance on you and your crime ring for the last several days. We know for a fact this party is just a cover for your attempt to snuff out your grandma. Don't get me wrong, nobody dislikes that old hag more than me, but being a good citizen requires I step in and save a life no matter how useless that life is."

Addressing the crowd again, she said, "This lowlife was going to snuff out his own granny and then pin it on one of you poor innocent folks. Now, there will be time for your praises and thanksgivings later, but right now we need to contact the police and get the garbage taken out." She looked at Bradley and raised her eyebrows when saying the word *garbage*, adding extra emphasis to what she thought of him.

Kaboom! Without notice, a loud explosion shook the ground, quickly followed by another, then another, then another…

Sylvia began shooting wildly in the direction of the noise, making a very strange pattern of bullet holes in the privacy fence.

Breathing hard and now in a crouched position, she looked towards the source of the noise. A very elaborate display of fireworks was filling the sky with color and sound.

"Oh, my bad," Sylvia apologized, but no one was really listening.

The impressive display of pyrotechnics brought the guests out from their hiding places to get a better look. Sylvia, also caught off guard, dropped her empty gun in her clutched hand to her side, watching the sparkles spreading across the sky.

Bradley saw his chance. To save the crowd from an elderly assassin, he lunged towards Sylvia and threw his handcuffed wrists over her neck like a calf being lassoed. The force of his body knocked her down. A big mistake on his part.

The moment the two of them hit the ground, Sylvia slipped out of the headlock and, in a flash, had his legs twisted up with hers. As she flipped him onto his back, she said, "Husband number 4 was a professional wrestler, so I know my way around a wrestling ring. Don't you be bringing that weak stuff over here, sissy boy! You are lucky I am out of bullets, or I would shoot you right now."

Bradley struggled to get free but with every move he made, her grip on his legs only got tighter. "Owww! You are going to break me in half! I can't feel my feet! Please let me go," he begged.

"Do you really think I am going to let you up?" Sylvia grunted, winded from the capture. "You broke my trust when you tried to tackle me, so now I have no other option but to squeeze your legs until they go to sleep. Once I have debilitated you, I am going to climb up on one of these tables, and just like a wrestler flying off of the top rope, I will jump down on you and flatten you like a pancake."

Her threats were interrupted by the sound of guns being cocked, and a man's voice yelling, "Nobody move!"

Once again, the harassed crowd of birthday party attendees threw their hands in the air, remaining motionless until given further directions.

Sylvia released her leg lock and started screaming, "I got him! I got the bad guy! Are the TV crews here?" She jumped to her feet and began fluffing her hair for her big moment, taking extra care to unstick the strays that were plastered onto her forehead by the remaining gloppy, camouflage foundation. "Where is that camera man? Make sure he spells my name right. It is *S-Y-L-V-I-A.*" She adjusted her top as she looked around for the television crew.

"Ma'am, put your hands in the air!" Officer Larry demanded.

Sylvia looked up at him and said, "Settle down, Mr. Crankypants. I have done my civic duty, and you are not going to come in here now and steal my thunder."

"Sylvia, you are in a lot of trouble, and you are under arrest, so you may want to be a little nicer to me."

"I am under arrest? But he is the mobster. I am the hero." She pointed to Bradley, who was still lying on the ground, trying to refill his lungs with air now that she had gotten off him.

She continued, "Maggie? Where are you? Come over here and tell these nice, handsome law enforcement officers the whole story." Sylvia pointed at her accomplice. "She can confirm everything."

Maggie had her hands in the air, refusing to move anything except her head, which she was adamantly shaking side to side.

Sylvia huffed and said, "Well, I refuse to be treated like a common criminal when it is very obvious I just saved a woman's life. I don't have to put up with this kind of treatment. I am offended, and I am leaving. Come on, Maggie, let's go."

She began walking towards the gate when Officer Larry shouted, "Sylvia, this is your last warning. Don't move or we will have to use force to restrain you."

Sylvia turned around and looked him in the eyes, pointing her finger in his face. "Now, listen here, young man, you better respect your elders."

She turned, took another step, and Officer Larry gave the command, "Taze her!"

Before Sylvia could respond, the assisting police officer laid a small black device on her shoulder, immediately dropping her to the ground. She flopped for a couple seconds, quivered, and began to drool.

Maggie ran to the aid of her friend. "Oh, my goodness, you killed her!"

"Please stay put, young lady," the officer warned her. "She is just fine."

"I need to save my friend." Maggie fell at Sylvia's side and began doing CPR chest compressions that were neither necessary, nor done correctly.

"This is your last warning, little lady. Step back or face the consequences!"

Maggie, learning nothing from Sylvia's rebellion, also ignored the officer's pleas. She cried, "Come back to me, Sylvia. Don't go towards the light!" She grabbed Sylvia's face in her hands and began to shake her in an attempt to bring her around. "You promised me you wouldn't die today because your hair is a mess."

And with that, Maggie saw the light. The bright light one experiences when being tazed.

BUSTED

It didn't take long for Officer Larry to realize he had made a huge mistake putting both women in the same squad car. The moment the effects of the tazing diminished, Sylvia began harassing Maggie.

"You are such a scaredy-cat. I had to do all of the dirty work while you spent most of your time at the buffet, which, by the way, I did not get to partake of."

"Well, I may not have been so scared if you hadn't shot a million holes in an innocent wooden fence."

"You listen here, missy, at least one of us was willing to do what was necessary to serve and protect."

"Sylvia, you cannot consider yourself a protector when the only one we needed protection was from you!"

"Maggie, that hurt me deeply." Sylvia put on her best fake, manipulating sad face. "Not only have the police misunderstood my actions, but my best friend has also. I know the only reason you doubt me is because you are under the spell of Mr. Evil."

Sylvia leaned forward in the car seat, making sure the policeman could hear her clearly.

"We have proof that Bradley is a mobster, whether lovestruck Maggie will tell you about it or not."

Officer Larry interrupted, "Sylvia, you raided a surprise birthday party for a ninety-year-old woman. It was a birthday party, and that was all. Bradley is not a mobster. As a matter of fact, he is quite possibly the most law-abiding citizen I ever dealt with. He knew this party was going to be a big deal, so he came to us the moment he got in to town and informed us of all his plans. Everyone on the force knew the details of this party. He did everything by the book. He paid for the permit for the fireworks, he got permission to have all the cars park on the street, and he even hired my own mother to make the cake!"

"Oh, I love her cakes." Sylvia turned and told Maggie, "I dare you to find one that is as moist as hers. She makes a red velvet cake with cream cheese frosting that is so good, if you put a slice on top of your head, your tongue will beat your brains out trying to get to it."

Maggie replied, "Oh, a piece of cake does sound good right now. I am pretty hungry. I fixed my plate but never got to eat it. They had some crab-stuffed mushrooms that smelled delicious. I wonder if we could go back and get some?"

Officer Larry interrupted, "Ladies! Focus! There is more to this story, and you need to listen. Let's start with the big kicker. Bradley's father is not a mob boss. He is a big shot from Dallas, Texas. He owns several companies there and is a highly-respected businessman. He had Bradley doing the footwork for this party because he had a previous engagement. Would you like to know what that engagement was?"

"No, not really," Sylvia nonchalantly replied.

"Well, I am telling you anyway. He was not here because he was attending an awards banquet where the president of the United States honored him for his exceptional work with—of all things—the elderly!"

"Oh, that sounds nice." Sylvia tried to act interested, hoping to win some suck up points.

The officer looked at her in the rearview mirror and snarled at her insincerity then continued, "I should also let you know, because of his connections, there were several dignitaries in the crowd. You may remember that crowd… since you shot at them."

"Technically, I didn't shoot at them. I shot in the air."

"Sylvia, you threatened to shoot a man in the crotch." Officer Larry shook his head in disbelief. "I think you may have outdone yourself this time."

"So what do I need to do? Write an apology? Do community service like Lindsay Lohan? What?"

"Don't know what you can do to fix this one because right now there are too many charges to count. We are going to lock you up until the judge decides what he wants to do with you."

"I'm going to the pokey?" Sylvia said with a grin.

"Yes. You're going to the pokey," he cleared his throat. "I mean jail! Now be quiet and let me drive."

The rest of the ride to the station was quiet, except for the occasional sound of Maggie whimpering.

Booked, fingerprinted, and put in a holding cell, Sylvia began planning her future. "Now that I am a real gangsta, I will need a tattoo. I am thinking of getting the American flag inked across my lower back. Since the flag is the symbol of freedom, when the guards and other inmates see it, they will know that even if they hold my physical body captive, my soul will always be free." Pausing to imagine her new body art for a moment, she nudged Maggie. "What kind of tat are you getting?"

Maggie was lying on the bench, her face ghostly pale, her forearm draped across her forehead. "I think I'm going to throw up," she said, feebly.

"Lay there for a few minutes, and you'll be fine. Right now, we need to figure out who our one phone call is going to be." She began counting off her options. "None of my exes. Not my son. Definitely not my pastor. Can you think of anyone? What about your dad?"

"Are you kidding me?" Maggie sat straight up and glared at Sylvia. "What am I supposed to say? Hi, Dad, this is Maggie. I'm just in jail for shooting up an old lady's birthday party, holding a rich man hostage, extortion, and, quite possibly, indecent exposure because my rear end is still hanging out of the hole in my pants! Could you swing by and pick me up?"

"So you can't call your dad? Well, what about Mr. Gene then?" Sylvia said, oblivious to Maggie's devastation. "He's our only choice."

Sylvia got up from the wooden bench and began shouting down the hallway, "We have our rights! We get one phone call, and if someone does not get us a phone right now, we are going to contact Judge Judy and report this police brutality."

The jailer came strolling towards the cell where the ladies were being held. "Sylvia, calm down. We were just waiting for your bail to be set. You can make your phone call."

"That's more like it. Maggie, go with him and get somebody to spring us from this joint."

The jailer unlocked the door, and Maggie stepped free, giving her baggy pants a tug. She followed him down the hallway to an empty desk with only a telephone sitting on it.

"There you go, little lady," the jailer pointed to the phone.

"Thank you, sir. This is my first crime, so I am a little unsure of the etiquette when it comes to making a call for bail."

"Well there is a phone book in the top drawer if you need it."

"I won't need it. The number I am about to call, I know as well as my own name."

The jailer stepped to the side of the room while Maggie dialed the restaurant. Mr. Gene answered.

"Hello, Mr. Gene. This is Maggie. I am sorry to bother you, but I have a teeny, tiny, itty, bitty issue, and you always told me to call if I needed something, remember?"

Mr. Gene's voice was deep, and his words were chosen carefully. "What in the world did you do now? And by any chance is Sylvia also having a teeny, tiny, itty, bitty issue?"

"Funny you should ask. Yes, she is with me, and if you were to guess that we were in jail you would be right. Haha, isn't that funny?" Maggie was trying hard to make light of the situation, but the moment she finished the sentence, she started chewing on her bottom lip in hopes of keeping herself from crying.

"I am on my way," he said sternly, not waiting for a reply before slamming the receiver down, leaving Maggie in silence.

Tears pooled up in her eyes, and her lip began to quiver. Not being able to be brave any longer, she laid her head on the desk and began sobbing.

"Here, here, now," the jailer said, awkwardly patting her on the shoulder. "I am sure it is going to be all right. I mean, no one is dead, right?"

Maggie lifted her head and looked at the man. "That is the best you got?"

"Yeah, I am not very good at the mooshy stuff. Maybe we should get you back to Sylvia. She might be better at it than I am."

"A rabid pit bull has more compassion than she does."

"I would agree with you on that point," he replied.

Maggie just got settled in her cell when the jailer returned. "Okay, you are free to go."

Sylvia jumped up and ran to the door. "It's about time. I'm starving."

"Oh, sorry. Not you. The man at the desk only paid Maggie's bail."

"Well, that dirty old scum-sucking pig. How dare he! I knew he did not like me, but this is inhumane."

Maggie offered to help. "I will go talk to him and see if he might go ahead and make an exception."

"Nope. I got it under control. I will call Mr. Newsome. That man would sell his house if I asked him to get me out of here. Just call me later."

Maggie threw her arms around Sylvia's neck in a tight embrace before stepping out of the cell, the jailer shutting the door behind her. Sylvia said, "Mags, don't worry. I will get us out of this mess. I always do."

Maggie nodded at her before putting one foot in front of the other, taking the longest walk of her life. Turning the corner, there was Mr. Gene, a familiar scowl on his face, standing by the front door. Knowing he was going to yell at her did not deter her in the least. She ran to him and threw her arms around his waist, burying her head into his chest. Tears flowed down her face as she tried to explain, "Oh, Mr. Gene, please know I did not shoot anybody."

"I know," he said, softened by her contrite attitude. "I already talked to Officer Larry, and he told me everything. Now dry your face off and get in the car. We will talk about it later."

There were no words spoken on the drive to Maggie's house, and when they arrived, she graciously thanked him, kissing him on his chiseled cheek before getting out of the car.

"I don't know what I would do without you. I love you very much." she said.

"I feel the same about you. Now get out of here." Overcome by his own feelings, he turned and looked out the window so she wouldn't see him wipe the tear from his eye.

She got out of the car, and walked slowly into the house, dreading the conversation she was about to have with her daddy.

The TV was blaring, which was typical during her father's Saturday afternoon nap time. Maggie could barely hear the gardening show being broadcast over the sound of his snoring. *If I wake him and tell him this story, it will upset him and possibly cause a heart attack. I think I will wait until he is well rested, then I can break it to him gently,* she thought.

Stepping lightly to avoid making the steps squeak, she got to her bedroom and threw herself on the bed, exhausted. Analyzing the events of the day, she focused on Officer Larry's explanation. A smile crossed her face as she realized, "Wait a minute! So Bradley is a good guy. I knew it!" Her smile quickly melted as she reminded herself, "So that's just great. I finally found a nice guy I like, but he will never know how I feel because I have royally blown it. There is no way in the world his father will let him date a girl who is in prison."

She pulled out a small piece of stationery from her nightstand and lay back down on the bed to write Bradley a note. "I at least owe him an apology before he leaves town. I am sure he will get all of the details of this fiasco at our trial, but there are some personal details I need him to know."

Nervously chewing on her ink pen, trying to figure out where to start, she wondered, *How does one go about apologizing for handcuffing a person without cause?*

Trying to come up with the right words, she laid her head down to rest her eyes and immediately fell asleep from exhaustion, the small piece of paper beside her, which read only, "Dear Bradley."

FORGIVENESS, SEALED WITH A KISS

THE RINGING OF the doorbell startled Maggie from her nap. Assuming it was Officer Larry, she stood up and listened at the door, hoping he would be the one to tell her father all about the day's events so she wouldn't have too. She quickly realized the man's voice she was hearing wasn't the officer's. It was Bradley's.

She ran from her room, making it down the flight of stairs two steps at a time. "Maggie!" her father yelled. "You have a visitor." He turned in anticipation of her arrival, but before he steadied himself, she was already standing beside him. Her sudden appearance caused him to let out a startled yelp. "Well, there you are," he said. As he focused on his daughter, a puzzled expression came across his face. He squinted his eyes and leaned closer to get a better look. Reaching up, he gently pulled the apology note she had been working on before her nap from her cheek; the drool that had run from her mouth while she slept made for a great adhesive.

He handed the damp note back to her and said, "I think I need a snack. I'll leave you two kids alone. It was nice to meet you." He shook Bradley's hand before disappearing into the kitchen.

Her father's exit provided a silence between Bradley and her that greatly increase her anxiety. It took all the strength she had to gain the confidence to raise her gaze, and once she caught his eye, she didn't know whether to throw her arms around him and hug him or throw herself to the ground and beg for mercy. They both began to speak at the same time. Maggie stopped. "You go, first."

"No, you go ahead," Bradley replied.

Maggie was about to burst, so she took the invitation. "I am so nervous, and I don't know where to begin. I mean, this is my first crime, and I do not know what the appropriate apology for a felony is."

Bradley's grin returned to his face, but this time, it upset Maggie.

"I don't know why you're smiling. This is serious. I'm about to be sent down the river for the rest of my life, and this may be the last time I see you face-to-face before I am sitting in the courtroom with a jury of my peers. Please listen carefully and take every word I say very seriously."

Once the words began, they ran out of her mouth as fast as a third-grade class going out for recess. "I need to start my apology for something that happened all the way back to the first day I met you. When you and your father came into the diner and began talking about Mrs. Jensen, Sylvia and I eavesdropped on your private conversation and that was when we overheard you talking about killing your grandmother, or so we thought. From that point on, our imaginations ran wild."

"I know," he said, but she continued.

"And then I need to apologize for breaking into your hotel room. Oh, and seeing your underwear. I now know that was wrong, and we should have went to the police."

"I know. I talked to Sylvia."

Maggie didn't hear a word he had said, and she continued. "I am sorry for thinking your family were mobsters. That was rude, and I am usually a nice person, but I got all caught up in wanting to get an award from the mayor, so my dad would be proud of me, and the next thing you know, I became the one who was the criminal."

"Maggie!" he snipped. "I know. Please listen." His face was gentle and kind as he continued, "Sylvia called me and told me she was the one to blame, that you just went along with her, doing her dirty work. She explained how you kept saying you thought I was really a nice guy, but she refused to listen because she really wanted to be on Oprah. I'm not quite sure what she meant by that, but she did verify that you really had no part in it. She also wanted me to know how much she cared about you, and if anything ever happened to you, she couldn't live with herself. I'm a bit sappy, so I told her if she would be totally honest with me, I would see what I could do. That was when she told me everything."

"Everything?" Maggie asked.

"Yes. Everything. After she honestly answered all of my questions, I went and met with my father, my grandmother, and Officer Larry."

"By any chance did Officer Larry mention how long of a sentence they were thinking about giving me? I need to let Mr. Gene know as soon as possible, so he can hire a temp to fill my position until I get back."

"You are not going to jail. I had the charges dropped at Grandmother's request. Apparently, she thinks this was the best birthday she's ever had."

Maggie looked at him and said, "Please don't tease me. Usually, I like a good practical joke, but I just don't have much of a sense of humor today."

"No, I'm serious. Since the shooting, her phone has rung off the hook. She is the most popular woman in town. All of the ladies in her bridge club are calling, wanting to hang out with her because they think she is famous. As a matter of fact, she asked me if I could see if you and Sylvia would come by one day this week and have your photo taken with her. She wants to take it to bingo so she can tell her friends how she was "shot at by a lunatic" on her birthday. Those were her words, not mine"

Maggie replied, "No offense taken. But let me get this clear. So I'm not going to have to make license plates in prison?"

Bradley giggled, "No, you're not going to prison. But, there is something else I need to talk to you about."

"Oh no, here it comes." Maggie said. She felt a rush of blood go to her head in anticipation of bad news. "I fully understand you never want to speak to me again." She looked down at the ground and dug her toe into the carpet, bracing herself for what she was about to hear.

"Actually, it's quite the opposite. Since my grandmother is getting older, my father has asked me to relocate my business here and keep an eye on her. Originally, I wasn't up for the idea, but now I have the proper motivation." He hesitated. "That motivation is you."

Maggie's head popped up so quickly, she grabbed her neck in pain. "Oww!" she yelped. "I think I just threw my neck out."

"Are you okay?"

She smiled ear to ear while still holding her head in her hand. "If what you are telling me is true, I will be just fine. Are you really staying here?"

"Yes. In between party planning, I found an apartment over on Mark Twain Street. I am going to my place in the city this weekend to pack my things, but I should be back here by Monday."

Maggie swallowed hard and said the only words she could speak, "That's nice."

"I will be busy unpacking Monday, but I was sure hoping you would be able to go to dinner with me on Tuesday."

"Like a…date?"

"Yes. A date."

"Well, since you are not blowing up old people, I would love to go out with you." She felt her face get warm again, but this time, she didn't feel like she was about to faint.

"Great. I hate to rush off, but Grandmother is waiting for me to take her dress shopping. She thinks with all of her newly-found popularity, she needs some new threads. She also said something about not wanting to look like a schoolmarm. Not sure what that means, but I have to get going. I will call you when I get back in town."

"Okay," she ran to the desk in the dining room, grabbed a pen, and scribbled her phone number on the back of the unfinished apology note her father had plucked from her face.

She reached out to hand it to Bradley, but he reached beyond the paper and took hold of her hand, not letting go. Nervously, she shook his hand as if they had just completed a business meeting. She tried to let go, but he continued to hold on, slowly and tenderly pulling her closer to himself.

She looked up into his eyes. *This is it*, she thought. *The kiss I have dreamed about.*

In her excitement, she closed her eyes a little early and lunged forward, underestimating the distance between them. Their faces met with such force, their teeth clinked together causing them to both recoil in pain.

"Sorry, I am new at this, and—"

He took his hand and softly put it to her lips. "Shh, you hold still, and let me show you how this is done." His words were like a cold breeze on her skin, causing goose bumps to run from her head to her toes.

As if it was happening in slow motion, he came closer until his lips finally came into contact with hers. Maggie saw fireworks more spectacular than the ones at Mrs. Jensen's party. He slowly pulled away, but her eyes remained closed, savoring the moment.

"Maggie," he said.

"Yes?" she replied, eyes still closed.

"I will see you Tuesday."

She opened her eyes and dreamily replied, "Thank you."

He smiled, tousled her ponytail, and walked out the door, closing it behind him.

"Thank you? I just said thank you for a kiss?" she scolded herself. "What a dork!" She smiled as wide as her lips would stretch. "But a dork that was just kissed by a beautiful man who is not a mobster!"